MOTH

A Novel

by Michael Takeda

**HOT REDHEAD
MEDIA**
ALL THINGS BOOKS AND LIT

HOT REDHEAD MEDIA
hotredheadmedia.com

Cover design by H. Zion

First Edition:

Identifiers: 978-1-7343052-7-2 (print) | 978-1-7343052-8-9 (ebook) |

This book is entirely a work of fiction. The names, characters and incidents portrayed in it are the work of the author's imagination. Any resemblance to actual persons, living or dead, events or localities is entirely coincidental.

PRAISE FOR MICHAEL TAKEDA:

Praise for Moth

"Vividly set in the walled city of Urbino, Italy – where a rich Renaissance history is blended with a gritty modern scene of drugs and sex – Michael Takeda's Moth follows a figurative lost soul into a more literal damnation. Moth is a dagger-sharp study of addiction, obsession, and self-destruction, wrapped in a mysterious cloak of the supernatural."
—Jeffrey Thomas, author of *Punktown*

"There are a lot of vampire novels coming out right now. So what readers need most are new explorations of the vampiric, of the monstrously sexual. Takeda's novel delivers exactly what is needed. Reading it feels as if Jim Carrol's The Basketball Diaries was puréed in a blender with some dank old vampire horror stories. What's red and golden and disturbing all over? This book right here."
—Raven Belasco, author of the Blood & Ancient Scrolls Series

Praise for Narcissus is Dreaming

"Narcissus is Dreaming is sensual as silk, sharp as a stiletto, and dark as the night itself. A provocative SF thriller that won't let you go."
—Allen Steele, author of *Coyote Rising*

"Narcissus is Dreaming reminds me of some of the work of the late Theodore Sturgeon, who also dealt with concepts of otherness, loneliness, and the endless varieties of love."
—Analog

"This quick, interesting sci-fi read takes us inside the emotions of a shape-shifter living among humans... Narcissus Is Dreaming is a straightforward account of reality with a twist."
—ForeWord Reviews

Praise for The Muses: The Blood Tour

"If you like your vampires sexy and scary in equal measure, your characters complex and involving, your plotlines engrossing and page-turning, then Michael Takeda has the recipe for you. The Muses is a tasty concoction indeed, but just remember this warning from one of its characters: 'Don't eat the groupies!'"
—Jeffrey Thomas, author of Blood Society and Punktown

"If you are searching for dark literature that is as grim as it is compelling, as beautiful as it is complex, you will find it in The Muses. The story, characters, and writing are unrelentingly haunting and sexy in equal measure. Takeda's hypnotic voice cannot be denied."
—John Edward Lawson, author of SuiPsalms

"Takeda's vampires are both cunning and beastly, deceptive yet heartfelt. His vividly painted creatures radiate a collage of emotions with which readers will instantly identify. Not since Poppy Z. Brite's Lost Souls has the literary vampire exuded and delivered such dark intentions and ultimate pleasures of the inhuman condition. The Muses draws blood...hard!"
—Andrew Wolter, author of Much of Madness, More of Sin

Dedication:

For all the gold-eyed monsters.

ONE

Our protagonist steps out of the movie theater into the night. The cool air whistling down the narrow, cobbled streets accosts him, shocking after the dark warmth of the cinema. Even more unsettling is the sensation that overcomes him every time he leaves after a particularly engrossing film, a sensation similar to nostalgia, in which he feels momentarily disoriented, obligated to adjust from the soothing lull of the celluloid world to the sharp bite of the reality that lies just beyond the theater door. He blinks a few times, hesitating outside the exit while happy couples and groups of young boys teasing each other push past him. Our protagonist has a tendency to slouch, although he would like to be taller, but occasionally he catches himself slumped forward and straightens his spine, only to lapse back into an unhealthy posture a few moments later. As he now straightens up, his gaze scans the dispersing crowd.

He finds no familiar faces, which causes a sudden and acute awareness that he is alone, which he finds uncomfortable if not painful. He steps forward, away from the crowd, his shoulders already slouching in his black leather peacoat, glancing at his watch, although he already knows it's around midnight, that it isn't too early to go to the club, and that he's got nowhere else to go.

Our protagonist has a name. Michael. A name common enough to warrant a nickname, of which he has several, but the one that stuck the hardest, came from a joke by a South Kensington boy during his time in London who called him Moth, because he only came out at night.

So Moth it was. His Italian friends here in Urbino had picked up on this right away. Moth: *Farfalla notturna* in Italian. Not that he really has any friends here. He has acquaintances. He's been away too long.

He's been away so long, in fact, that Italian, his first language, comes out stilted and flat, in the lazy American method of speech he absorbed during his youth in the Midwest and elsewhere in the States.

Moth is a pretty boy. He appears a few years younger than his actual age of twenty-eight. He is slim but muscular enough to not be considered scrawny. Currently he wears his dark brown hair at one length, in waves, to his shoulders, tendrils dyed with alternating black and red streaks. Other than his height, he is generally satisfied with his appearance except he dislikes his natural dark brown eyes, so he compensates with colored contact lenses: blue, green, or violet.

Moth fancies himself a rebel. This is most easily discerned by the extensive tattoo of a Chinese dragon in full color on his right arm that curls from his wrist, past his elbow, and over his shoulder to finish on his back. A series of piercings adorn both his ears. For a while he toyed with the idea of getting another tattoo: this time a moth on his bare left bicep. Not that a moth was a beautiful subject on the surface; really a moth was just an ugly little insect that would batter itself to death against a light bulb, too dumb to know the difference between the light bulb and the moon, but the idea appealed to him. Like the fragile butterfly, the moth started out as something else, transforming itself from a worm to a sturdy creature that could fly. Moth is fascinated by the idea of this transformation, a theme to which he returns repeatedly in his poetry, but he never got the tattoo.

Moth follows the already familiar path through the winding alleys to the club, affectionately referred to as *il Cesso* – which means The Dive or The Toilet – by the locals. It has another real name, one that Moth can't even remember. He discovered The Dive immediately after his return to Urbino, attracted to it instantly. It was the only club in all Le Marche that cultivated a gay clientele, and, besides that, had an extremely seedy reputation. Behind The Dive was a long, narrow, and windowless alley with an even worse reputation, where drugs, sex and money were regularly exchanged. Moth has his own name for the alley, which his friends (well, acquaintances) have enthusiastically adopted: Rats' Alley.

Moth borrowed the reference from T.S. Eliot's phenomenal work, *The Waste Land*: *I think we are in rats' alley / Where the dead men lost their bones.* He didn't bother to explain to them where he'd stolen the reference. It was Moth's empirical opinion that certain types of people, particularly in the crowds he often fell in with, were suspicious of you if you walked around with your head full of poetry, your own or someone else's. Of all the dangerous, shameful, and often illegal activities in which Moth had participated for more than a decade, poetry was his dirty little secret.

He reaches the door of The Dive. Loud and mindless techno music spills out into the street, rhythmic arrows shooting through his chest. He straightens his back and composes an expression of cool indifference before he enters. He descends the stairs that lead into the club proper, the noise level rising with every step. In Urbino, several bars are located underground, no space to build out, so everything expands down, literally an underground scene. This meant that The Dive was small, dark and labyrinthine, which served to accentuate its seediness. Moth's only complaint was the music. He would have preferred something darker and moodier. But at least this place existed, otherwise he would have died of boredom by now.

It's Saturday night. The place is crowded. Moth recognizes a few faces of the Saturday night crowd. Fags from Urbania, Pesaro, and all the little towns in-between make the weekly pilgrimage to The Dive, everybody looking for something.

Moth has been coming here for three months. For three months he has been in Urbino, since the end of December. He, too, is looking for something but can't quite put it into words. *A wordless poet, how sad,* he thinks to himself. If pressed, Moth will say that he's looking for inspiration. He's looking for his Muse. A boy who will inspire him to create sonnets, no, epic sagas, bigger than Eliot, bigger than Shakespeare, bigger than Walt Whitman. Thinking of Walt Whitman brings a poem by Allen Ginsberg to mind. Moth then realizes that he's standing in the middle of the club while everyone assesses then undresses him with their hungry eyes as he absentmindedly mumbles poetry to himself, so he moves toward the bar before he is approached. He doesn't want to be propositioned by any of these old leeches. That's all that Moth seems to get these days: old leeches. In all three months, he's only had one decent encounter at the club, a nineteen-year-old named Fabiano on leave from the military, whom Moth only saw once before the boy went back to his barracks. Other than that, it's been a dry winter.

At the bar, he yells for a beer. Waiting for it, he lets his eyes wander. He notices his friend Orazio (well, acquaintance, although the closest thing to a friend he has) further down the bar, talking to a leech. Orazio sees Moth and winks. Moth nods his head in greeting. A moment later, Orazio excuses himself from the leech, laying a very friendly hand on the leech's shoulder, and then slips over and squeezes into the small space next to Moth at the bar.

"*Ciao.*"

"*Ciao.*"

"What's happening?" Orazio asks.

Moth pays for his beer, takes a sip. "Not much."

Orazio glances back at the leech, then at Moth. "Have you got a cigarette?"

"No, I was going to ask you."

Orazio shrugs, and then reaches into his jean jacket, pulling out a pack of Marlboros. Moth accepts one along with a light from the silver Zippo in Orazio's quick, deft hands. Moth notices that Orazio's eyes are pinned but decides not to say anything. Orazio casts another quick glance behind him, drawing calmly on his cigarette. The leech is watching.

"Working?" Moth asks.

Orazio makes a vague gesture. "*Insomma,*" he says, one of those all-purpose Italian words that, in this case, apparently means *yes*.

"He's watching us," Moth remarks. "What did you say to him?"

Orazio's lips curl up into a charming smile, which changes his face completely from sullen sexuality to a boyish charm. "I told him I was going to the bathroom," Orazio says.

Moth shakes his head, faking disapproval. "You're a devil of a fellow," he says, one of his stock phrases frequently used to describe Orazio.

"I know," Orazio says, which is his usual response.

How quick we are to settle into patterns, Moth thinks, *and make up new habits.*

"I better go," Orazio says, gesturing at the leech.

"Will you be here tomorrow?"

"Sure," Orazio says. Then, "Kiss me."

Where?" Moth says, his tone insinuating.

Orazio makes the same vague gesture as before, then says, "On the cheek."

Moth leans forward and kisses Orazio on the cheek. Leaning back, he catches a glimpse of the lonely leech, eyes dark and expression grim. "Jealousy rears its ugly head," he says.

"See you later. *Ciao.*"

"*Ciao.*" Moth watches as Orazio slips his small, lithe body back through the crowd. With his big sincere smile, his flutter of charm, the leech is soon put at ease. All a part of the hustle. At twenty-one years of age, Orazio is young enough to make money hustling, but old enough to know what he can get away with. Moth has never hustled. The idea of sex for money has never done anything for him. Moth stubs out his cigarette. He should have bought a pack earlier, now he'll have to bum them. He glances back down the bar and sees Orazio leaving arm-in-arm with the leech. He wonders vaguely where they're going and what they will end up doing, if Orazio will spend the whole night with him while he, Moth, will most likely finish his beer and then start the long trek back to the shabby residence hotel where he will sleep alone.

At the end of the beer is when Moth sees *Him,* with a capital *H, a* man he's never seen before, a man so incredibly lovely in the classical sense, straight out of the Sistine Chapel, that Moth literally cannot stop staring at him. The Stranger glides through the crowd, looking about casually. He seems entirely aware that he is being watched, and not just by Moth. Moth is awestruck to the point of paralysis. The Stranger is tall, slim, and pale. High cheekbones. Aquiline nose. A noble brow. Long neck. Full lips. Thick black hair running like a river down the length of his back over a white silk shirt.

He is a dream made flesh, Moth thinks. The club is rather dark, so it's difficult for Moth to assess the Stranger's age with any accuracy, but something about the Stranger's confident carriage implies experience, putting him somewhere close to Moth's age. From his post at the bar, it's impossible to see the Stranger's eyes, but not impossible to see that the Stranger's eyes have now fallen on Moth, not only fallen upon him, but are now sweeping up and down slowly over Moth's body. Moth feels his heart stagger in his chest under the Stranger's too confident and too knowing gaze, still frozen in his chair. Then a small, smug smile creeps out from the corners of those full lips, his eyes still locked on Moth's eyes, and this smile causes Moth to become inexplicably aroused, all the blood draining in an instant from his heart to his dick. Then the Stranger breaks contact and moves toward the door.

For a moment, Moth tries to make sense of what has just happened. He thinks to himself: *There goes my muse,* and only then can he move. He grabs his coat without taking the time to put it on and pushes his way roughly through the crowd, ignoring the swears that slap his retreating back, up the stairs and out the door. He looks left, then right, but doesn't see the Stranger. He scans the street again, mentally kicking himself for his stupidity and inadequacy. He shivers in the shockingly cold air, slips into his coat, and resigns himself to the long walk home.

~

In another part of Urbino, beyond the Renaissance city walls, in a small but relatively new apartment, a young man sits alone in a double bed, pillows supporting his back. Surrounding him on the bed are several thick files and law books. He lazily scratches at the stubble on his jaw, contemplating what he has just read. Before he can come to any conclusions, he is interrupted by the rattle of a key in the lock of the front door. He takes off his reading glasses and sets them on the nightstand, waiting for her appearance.

She comes into the room, dropping her bag by the door. "Hey, baby," she says.

He smiles at her. "*Eh, la,*" he says.

Approaching him, her gaze roams over the mess on the bed. "Working?"

He makes a vague gesture. "*Insomma*," he says, meaning that he'd rather not.

She clears a space on the bed, then lies down on her side, head propped up on one hand. "I don't think there's enough room on this bed for the three of us."

He looks at her inquisitively. "The three of us?"

"Yeah," she replies, running a hand through loose, dark hair. "You, me and the law."

"Ah," he says, feigning disappointment. "I thought that you meant you and me and someone else," he says, gesturing down.

One of her dark, perfectly contoured eyebrows quirks up. "If I didn't know you better, I'd say you were trying to provoke me."

"I think you know me well enough."

They both laugh, but he sees that she is tired, so, as he reaches out to stroke her face, he changes the subject. "How'd it go?"

"All right," she says. She briefly describes the conference while he nods his head and makes noises of encouragement. Then she taps her fingers on one of his tomes. "You know, I think your lawyer is mean to you, giving you so much work."

He shakes his head. "This isn't for Luciano," he explains. "This is more personal."

"Would you care to share?"

"I've started doing some research on the side. About… Sex crimes."

"Hmm," she says. "Now you've got my full attention."

He studies her face. She has already taken off her glasses and looks at him attentively. He appreciates the fact that she always listens carefully to everything he says. Sometimes he thinks that she should have become a psychologist instead of a teacher even though she was extremely fortunate to find a teaching job so soon after graduating, and it was her money that was paying the rent. He had another year of his *pratica* before he could take the exam. And then, honestly, he wanted to rest. To take a break. Get away. He had studied his whole life. She agreed wholeheartedly with this. They had already dreamed up places where they could go. Hot places: Florida, Las Vegas, Mexico, Costa Rica, Cuba, Argentina. He hates the cold with a passion. Now that Spring is arriving, he feels himself growing lighter with the strength of the sun, his soul buoyed up like a bubble of air from the depths to the surface of the sea.

He rifles through the thick file on his lap. "I'm reading about this serial killer guy. He'd pick up women in discos, go home with them, have sex, and then poison them with high doses of narcotics, every four or five days, except for one time he went ten days.... Although, with his pattern, it's probable that there was another victim who just was never found." He glances at the file, innocently innocuous in its plain blue cover. "This was about ten years ago. In Rimini."

She knows that he used to travel out to Rimini to go dancing quite often a decade ago, when he was still just a teenager. "Lucky for you you're not a woman," she says, and he hums in agreement. "What happened to this guy?"

"He died before it even got to trial."

"How'd he die?"

"He OD'd on the same narcotics he used on his victims." He scratches at the stubble on his jaw again. "Better that he OD'd. Saved the taxpayers a lot of money."

"That's one way to put it," she says diplomatically.

"He was a sick bastard."

"I agree with you there," she replies. She stretches as she sits up, then she regards him with a teasing glint in her eye. "And this is how you spend your free time, with drug-addicted serial killers?"

He laughs. "I'd rather spend it with you."

"You're a sweet boy," she says as she rises. "But I'm beat. I'm going to take a shower and then go to bed."

"I'll have all this cleared off before you get back."

"Good idea," she says. At the bedroom door, she turns. "There's one thing I don't understand."

"What?"

"How did he convince all those women to go home with him?"

He grins at her. "Maybe he was good-looking like me."

"I doubt that," she says, and he watches with quiet appreciation as she saunters across the room, stretching her body, before disappearing past the threshold.

There were details of the case that he hadn't shared with her that made the case strange. The killer had used a one-hundred percent pure solution of heroin on his victims, no trace of any of the usual additives usually cut into the street version. The question was, where had it come from? No evidence had been found to answer this nor where the killer injected this, not in the arm, or neck, as would, perhaps, be expected, but the puncture wounds were found in the cervix. How, and, more importantly, why, as far as his curiosity was concerned, had also never been determined. *One sick bastard, this guy.*

The killer been in solitary confinement when he committed suicide by overdose. Someone must have smuggled the heroin in for him. They'd never discovered who it was, but they probably hadn't looked too hard.

The young, would-be lawyer closes up the file and starts piling books upon the floor. He's never thought of killing anybody. He is docile by nature, although he believes that he is capable of defending himself with violence, but only if it were absolutely necessary. He has never taken drugs. He never had an interest in them, and he believes that drugs are a refuge of the weak. He has, however, on one or two occasions when he was younger, gone home with a girl he'd just met at a discotheque. But even on those occasions, his motives had more to do with loneliness than with the plain desire to have sex.

These thoughts swirl through his mind like dead leaves in a gust of wind, as he tries to understand this case, but it's beyond his comprehension. He considers the question raised by his girlfriend: *How did he convince all those women to go home with him?*

A very good question, indeed.

TWO

Sunday night. Back to The Dive, then. In his ripped up Levis and a long-sleeved black shirt, Moth descends the stairs. He shrugs off his leather jacket as he looks around the room. Very few people tonight. He doesn't see Orazio, but he spots Juan sitting at a table in the corner with some pretty young guy with a familiar face. Juan gestures him over. Moth goes. They greet each other; Juan invites him to sit down and introduces him to the young guy. Moth knows Juan vaguely, through Orazio's brother Sam.

What Moth knows about Juan: he's been living in Urbino for about three years, originally from Spain. He's bisexual. He doesn't use any drug stronger than alcohol. This is all that Moth knows about him. Big guy, broad in the chest, tough looking; but, according to Sam, that was just an act.

"Have you seen Orazio?" Moth asks.

"No, haven't seen him."

"Who?" asks the boy companion.

"Orazio," Juan says.

"Oh," says the boy with a tone of disgust.

Juan leans closer. "Maybe he went to Rimini."

Moth considers this. It would be just like Orazio to say one thing and then do another. "It's possible."

"Everything's possible," Juan says philosophically. "But have you checked Rats' Alley?"

How interesting, Moth thinks, that he's influenced this. "He wouldn't have a reason to be in Rats' Alley."

Juan shrugs. "Then maybe he really is in Rimini."

"Who?" says the boy, having missed a part of the conversation.

"Orazio," Juan repeats.

"*Ancora*," mutters the boy. "Come on, let's get out of here. I'm sick of this place."

"If you want," Juan says. He downs the rest of his drink, salutes Moth, and leaves the club with his friend.

Moth muses over the boy's reaction. He must have gotten burned by Orazio. Well, no Orazio. He glances at his watch although he knows that it's about ll:30. Moth has a very accurate internal clock. In fact, he never wore a watch until he received this one as a gift. His watch is a Movado: very black, very beautiful and expensive. It's the only thing of value that he has left, having lost or sold the rest. Moth was in love with a man once, the man who gave him this watch. For this reason, he wears it always. Every time that he looks at this watch, he is reminded of this man and the three years that they spent together, and he is reminded of how he fucked it all up and lost him. Sometimes, in his more pessimistic moments, Moth thinks that all he is capable of is fucking things up.

He lights a cigarette and orders a beer from the passing waiter. *Maybe Orazio will show up later,* he thinks, but he knows that's not why he came. He came in hope of seeing the Stranger again, even though he is aware that it is unlikely. The Stranger has been in his thoughts almost non-stop, all day. Moth finds himself constantly fantasizing all kinds of little scenarios, mostly sexual, between him and the Stranger. His favorite fantasy involves the Stranger coming to him silently, not speaking a word at all, just looking at Moth with his green eyes – or blue, both work for the fantasy, smiling that odd little smile, putting his pale hands on Moth's belt, and then–

"Six thousand lire," says the waiter.

Moth looks at the waiter. "Let me ask you a question. You know about Marx? He said that religion was the opiate of the masses. If it's true that religion is the opiate of the masses, then what are opiates?"

The waiter scowls at him. "In this bar, you buy your drinks with cash, not philosophy."

Moth pays for the beer and lights up another cigarette. Maybe… maybe nothing.

He drinks the beer slowly. It tastes like water. He'd rather... he'd rather nothing.

He touches the little notebook that he always carries in his coat pocket. He'd tried earlier to write something, but was unsuccessful. He withdraws the little notebook and flips through it, reading at random. Usually, he doesn't write in bars. People consider writing in a bar to be an open invitation to ask about what he's writing, and generally stick their nose in his business. But Moth doesn't know what else to do with himself. He can't even finish a thought without it turning as sour as old milk mixed with new lemons. The page opens up before him. He reads what he had tried to write about the Stranger, not poetic:

"I've heard it said about some people that they radiated sensuality. Or in some cases, they say 'sexuality' when they mean 'sensuality.' Take O, for example. He is sexy, but he doesn't radiate shit. Exploits it, of course. But *He* radiated sexuality. He wore his sexuality like a halo over his entire body. An angel of sex."

A voice interrupts Moth's concentration. "What are you writing about?"

Moth looks up, annoyed, a snappy retort about how he was reading, not writing, and *what the hell is it to you* on the tip of his tongue, which immediately melts away when he sees that it is the Stranger, *Him*, standing in front of Moth's table. In fact, Moth becomes speechless, staring stupidly at the Stranger.

The Stranger has gold eyes.

The Stranger casually brushes a loose lock of black hair from his pale cheek and gives Moth that odd little smile, which has the same effect as it had the night before. "I mean, what are you reading?" he says. His voice is a deep melody. "Something you wrote?"

Yeah, about you, my muse, Moth thinks, but what comes out is, "Nothing." *Shit!* Moth reprimands himself mentally. *Michael, you fucking idiot...*

"Nothing?" the Stranger says, his tone playful. "How interesting." He reaches down and takes one of Moth's cigarettes from the pack on the table. "Well, good luck with your 'nothing'," he says, then turns and glides away into the crowd.

Stupid! Stupid! Stupid! "Wait," Moth says, but not loud enough to be heard over the music. He jumps up, grabs his coat, and follows the Stranger with the gold eyes.

The Stranger heads out the back of the club, straight into Rats' Alley. The alley is dark, lined with alcoves that are even darker. Moth has lost sight of the Stranger, so now he walks slowly through the alley, staring into the recesses, searching. An irate boy in an intimate moment calls out, *What the fuck are you looking at?* but Moth continues on undaunted, toward the end of the alley.

A cry in the dark shatters the relative silence. "Cops!" someone shouts. Anyone involved in criminal activity, which was everyone, now scatters out either end of the alley. Some manage to slip out, but nearly everyone is apprehended by the river of policemen pouring in. Moth sees that it is too late for him to escape, so he backs up into one of the alcoves, moving quickly. He crouches down, tugging up the left leg of his jeans to grab what he's hiding in his boot, but, before he can manage, a bright light blinds him, and two pairs of arms with disembodied voices beyond the light saying, "No, you don't" and "Come here, you bastard" seize hold of him, dragging him to his feet and then down to the police van beyond the alley.

THREE

Moth doesn't make any friends in jail. After an unpleasant strip search, he is locked up and forgotten about for the rest of the night. He refuses to let himself cry, though he isn't far from it. They've taken his personal items, of course, which consisted of the Movado watch, his recently acquired *carta d'identità*, a few thousand lire, and his notebook. His notebook in someone else's hands frustrates him most of all. At least he had written in English. He doubts that any of these *paesini* cops could read it if they tried. So he passes the night, cursing his luck, unable to write, trying not to think about Mr. Gold Eyes, and being generally pissed off to the point where the others in the cell decide it best to leave him alone.

In the morning, they remember him. They take him out of the cell into a barren room where an officer, not much older than Moth, sits behind a desk, studying Moth's *carta d'identità* carefully and thoughtfully like it was a text by James Joyce. The officer that escorted Moth tells him to sit down, and then goes around to the other side of the desk beside the reader.

Finally, still looking at the *carta d'identità*: "Gallo, Michele."

"*Si*," Moth says.

"Place of birth: Urbino."

"*Si.*"

"Place of residence: Via di San T—, 84, Urbino," he reads.

Technically, not true. But to get the card, he needed a real address. "It's my brother's address," Moth says.

This leads to a lengthy discussion about where Moth actually lives. He gives the police a story about staying with his brother until he finds a place of his own. He doesn't understand what all the fuss is about. His parents, then? In America. And his brother, what does his brother do for a living?

Moth hesitates a moment although he doesn't know why. "Lawyer."

The officers look at each other, and one says something in a low voice to the other. Then the one standing leaves the room. The remaining officer studies Moth for so long that the silence in the room becomes a tangible though insubstantial presence, like a ghost. "Luciano Gallo is your brother?" he asks finally.

Moth is tired. He hasn't slept. "Yes," he says wearily.

"He's a good man, your brother," the officer says with the implicit reproach that he, Moth, is not so good. *So be it.* "Does your brother know that you use drugs?" Moth figures that the question is rhetorical, so he remains silent. "I'm sure he does know. Aren't you ashamed of yourself?" More rhetoric. The officer holds up the loaded syringe that they'd pulled out of Moth's boot the night before. "Don't you know that this will kill you?"

Maybe that's the point, Moth thinks. He sees that, this time, the officer awaits a response. What can Moth say? That he's hurting no one but himself? That he's tried to stop but can't? That it's nobody's business but his own? That he only uses occasionally? That the syringe wasn't his, it was somebody else's? That he's just a sick junky bastard? What is true and what isn't? What is truth worth? What the hell does this cop want?

Moth averts his eyes. "Yeah, I know," he says.

The cop's tone lightens a little. "You know, they have places for boys like you."

Boys like you. "Yeah, I know."

One cop approaches and speaks softly to the other. Then the first tells Moth that they talked to his brother. Moth flinches and the cops seem to enjoy his sudden discomfort. The cop says that they'll release Moth, on the condition that he goes directly to the office of his brother. They ask him if he can make it on his own, or do they have to escort him there?

Moth considers the escort just to save himself the trouble of the walk, but the mental image of the cruiser pulling up at his brother's office, with him in it, is not appealing.

"I can make it on my own," he says.

~

At the law office of Gallo and Fiesta, Moth finds himself waiting in the front office while his brother Luciano is in a private conference with a client. At least that's what the paralegal told him when he arrived. Other than Moth and the paralegal, there's no one else in the room. There's not much to look at in the front office: a desk, a couple of chairs against the wall, a few law degrees in frames, a Raphael print, and the young paralegal behind the desk. Moth has no interest in the degrees or in Raphael, so he lets his eyes settle on the young man.

He's seen this guy around town, recognizes his face from somewhere. Maybe he's seen him in that café in Piazza della Repubblica, Moth doesn't remember where exactly, but he's certain that he's never talked to this guy before today. While the paralegal is engrossed in a file that he's reading, Moth takes a good look. Short, dark hair curling wildly. A sharp, strong jaw that could cut glass. A mouth shaped well. He has smooth hands with long fingers, nice hands. As he reads, he lifts his index finger and presses it to his lips, deep in concentration. Eyes downcast, Moth can only see the dark eyelashes which fan themselves out forever. About three days of dark stubble on his face give him a solid air of masculinity. All together, he's a good-looking man.

Moth continues to watch. There is something he finds intriguing in the act of watching someone who doesn't realize that they are being watched. He starts thinking that he could write a poem about this guy, if he weren't so tired.

The paralegal closes the file, gets up, and puts it away in the cabinet. Moth follows him with his eyes. Under a loose gray sweater and well-tailored blue jeans, he's slim. Not much taller than Moth, maybe. Good posture. Moth can tell by his walk that he's as straight as a post. He returns to the desk with another file, glancing at Moth as he sits down. He has green eyes.

Moth decides to speak. "You work here long?"

The paralegal with green eyes takes a good look at Moth. He doesn't like to judge people without knowing them, but he has a strong suspicion that this guy is a loser. In fact, he's seen this guy before, twice at Basili's and once in the piazza, hanging out with the local addicts. Urbino is not a big town, everyone knows who the junkies are. He also suspects that this one was the one the police called Luciano about, so no good news here. Probably busted for drugs. And even if he's not a drug addict, he's certainly trying to make a bad impression with his jeans torn to pieces and the multicolored hair. It was hard to meet any good people in a law office, *che gente*. But there's no need to be unprofessional, so he answers in a polite tone of voice. "About a year."

This guy's an icicle, Moth thinks. "You like it?"

The paralegal hesitates. He doesn't really want to be dragged into this conversation. "It's interesting."

"Oh, really?" Moth asks. "You find the law interesting?"

"I studied it for ten years," he says. He speaks slowly, clearly and precisely, like an educated man should, without a hint of the local dialect. "I guess that means yes."

"You guess?" Moth says.

This guy is annoying. Hoping to shut him up, the paralegal says, "And what do you do?"

"Unemployed."

The paralegal doesn't find that surprising.

"I've seen you around," Moth says. The paralegal doesn't respond. "What's your name?"

"Arturo."

Moth doesn't have to guess that this guy does not like him, nor does he give a shit. He gives the paralegal a long look of disbelief and says, "You're kidding."

What? Arturo loses all patience and fixes him with a cold and penetrating stare that actually startles Moth. He's about to say something less than professional when the door behind him swings open, and Luciano's client walks out. The intercom buzzes, Luciano brusque:

"Send Michael in."

Moth gets up from the chair, forces a trite smile at Arturo, and goes in.

Che gente!

Luciano was already thirteen years old when Moth was born. For thirteen years, Luciano was an only child, a mixed blessing. The family had been two steps above poor. Their paternal grandfather had been a *contadino* – a farmer, and unable to help his son financially. On their mother's side, it hadn't been much better. Luciano remembers these times clearly. There was rarely meat on the table, and he went through childhood wearing second-hand clothes. Of course, at the time, he hadn't been aware of how poor they were, another mixed blessing.

In retrospect, Luciano knows that these lean times left an impression on him. From this poverty, he's come away with frugality, compassion, a respect for hard work and independence, and a strong sense of the value of money.

Moth, on the other hand, was born when the family was moving out of its poverty. He was born when and because their parents could afford him. When Luciano was eleven, their father had found work with a leather goods company and was soon making decent money. Their parents were hopeful for the future. Moth was the baby of the future. For this, he was spoiled terribly.

Luciano studies his brother in the office now, thinking these thoughts. Perhaps Moth turned out this way because he's been spoiled, had had everything given to him, every whim satisfied, and hadn't learned anything about responsibility. Maybe the fact that their father had often been away from home, traveling due to his job, had also had an influence on Moth's emotional development. Boys need fathers.

Moth shifts in his chair. He expected a lecture from his brother; instead, he has to sit here while Luciano looks at him with his hound-dog eyes full of disappointment, which is, somehow, a lot worse. He reaches over to the desk for the ashtray – although Luciano doesn't smoke – and lights up his last cigarette to mask his unease. Too much silence. "Well?" Moth says.

Luciano has been considering what to say. He has calmed down considerably since the phone call from the station. Due to the difference in their ages, he's always felt protective of Moth. "What happened?"

A vague question, which has nothing to do with last night. "What do you mean?"

"I think you know what I mean."

Moth smokes. "I don't know," he says. "I don't know what happened."

Luciano considers this tendency of his brother to be introverted. Even as a child, Moth was very reserved. Getting a straight answer out of him has always been difficult. "Where did you get it?"

He'd gotten it from Orazio, a fair amount for a fair price. When Orazio scored big, he supplemented his income by selling off the extra. "From a friend."

"You have nice friends," Luciano says.

Moth doesn't say anything.

"Are you aware of how much trouble you're in?" Luciano asks.

Moth doesn't say anything.

Luciano folds his hands before him on the desk. "When the police called, I said that I'd take responsibility for you. They want you to talk to a social worker. I've already made an appointment for you tomorrow at eleven." He ignores the face that Moth makes. Moth hates social workers more than cops. "Next Monday you'll go down and see the judge. I'll go with you. If you show him you're serious about staying away from drugs, you can keep yourself out of too much trouble." Moth makes an even worse face. He hates judges even more than social workers. "Since I'm responsible for you, I've decided it best if you stay with us for a while."

Moth doesn't like the idea. "I've already paid the hotel until the end of the month."

Luciano glances at the calendar on his desk. "That's only three days."

"It's money wasted."

"We will give you a place to sleep and enough to eat. You won't need any money. End of discussion," Luciano says firmly, and then waits for Moth's response. There is none. "I'll take you over to the hotel now to get your clothes, and then I'll bring you home. Let's go."

~

At Luciano's house, Moth falls asleep on the sofa. He sleeps all afternoon and wakes up at eight o'clock in the evening. Luciano's wife has left him some dinner in the kitchen, which he picks at while she washes the dishes. Also at the kitchen table is their daughter, a beautiful six-year-old with big, dark eyes inherited from Luciano, named Giovanna. Giovanna Gallo. Joking around, Moth calls her Joe Low. Now the child is doing her schoolwork, eating cookies with milk, and keeping an attentive eye on her uncle.

Making sure that she's looking, Moth slowly snakes a hand across the table to steal a cookie from her plate. She stops writing, watching him. He bites the cookie, making an exaggerated sound of pleasure. "Mmmmm…"

She giggles. Her mother turns to see what's going on. "Are you finished?"

Joe Low gives Moth a knowing glance. "Almost," she says and continues writing.

Luciano's wife says to Moth, "Would you like a coffee?"

"No thanks," Moth says. When she turns away, he steals another cookie, this time making an even bigger sound of pleasure. "Mmmmmmmm…"

The child giggles again. Then she whispers, "Uncle," and takes a cookie, biting it, and imitating Moth. "Mmmmm…"

Moth goes out onto the terrace to smoke one of the cigarettes that Luciano had somewhat reluctantly bought him. He stares out at the cool dark, thinking. At one point he looks at his watch. It's early but he's not going anywhere. Monday night, The Dive is closed anyway. He doesn't feel comfortable at his brother's house. He's been here a few times, having been invited for dinner, but this apartment makes him restless. Too clean, too domestic, too normal. He thinks about writing a poem, but he doesn't feel like he can write in this heavy atmosphere of normalcy.

Moth goes back inside. Joe Low has finished her homework. "Uncle, play with me," she orders.

"Sure thing, sweet thing," Moth says in English. She laughs. For some reason she finds it humorous when he speaks English. Actually, she finds everything humorous. The joy of being six years old. Moth tries to remember what it was like to be that age. His family was still in Urbino. He remembers school. His best friend was a boy named Daniele who lived in the apartment building on the other side of the street. There were two other boys who lived nearby who always came out to play, but Moth's recollection of them is hazy. He remembers that their main idea of fun was to play soccer, two on two. He tries to remember these other boys, but their names and faces escape him. He doesn't know what happened to Daniele. He could still be here in Urbino. Actually, it was probable. And the other boys, too. Moth considers asking Luciano. Luciano would remember. But Moth decides against it. It's been twenty years since he knew these boys. He doesn't know them anymore, and it wouldn't do any good to see them again.

Joe Low grabs him by the finger and leads him to her room to play. They end up collaborating on an elaborate play performed with finger puppets. In this play, there's a mean dinosaur who roams around the countryside, eating all the little animals that he comes across—Joe Low insists on being the dinosaur, leaving Moth to beg for his life before being eaten--until a good fairy with gossamer wings comes down and convinces the bad dinosaur to change his ways, so he spits up all the animals that he's swallowed and they're all happy in the end, dancing and singing. Then, with slight variations, she makes Moth do it all over again.

Moth doesn't mind. He likes children.

He knows that he'll never have any of his own, a fact that disturbs his mother more than it does him. It was shortly after the birth of Joe Low that Moth came out of the closet to his mother. Not, of course, to his father. Even at twenty-two, he was still afraid of his father. Moth figured that since Luciano was now producing grandchildren, it would soften the blow, and he was tired of making excuses about why he never brought any love interest home to meet his parents. Moth remembers the conversation clearly. He was in the kitchen at his parents' house when she asked him the usual question.

"Michael, why don't you ever bring a nice girl home?"

Tired, Moth had finally given her the truth. "Because there aren't any girls, Ma. I'm gay."

His mother's calm, if not relieved, response: "I knew it."

Moth's sister-in-law comes in soon after to insist that the child go to bed. Joe Low refuses. She would rather play with her uncle. Moth has a fleeting thought: *Too bad I'm not this popular with the boys.* The child is put to bed anyway.

Nine-thirty in the evening. Moth finds a book by Baricco on the shelf, settles himself into a corner and starts reading. He remains undisturbed until just after eleven, when his brother wishes him a good night. Moth finishes the book and puts it on the floor. He thinks. The house is silent. Moving quietly, Moth goes over to his backpack and takes out his shaving kit. Then he takes the cigarettes and his lighter from the kitchen table. While he's in the kitchen, he also picks up half a lemon from the fridge. Then he goes to the bathroom and locks himself in.

He opens up his shaving kit and takes out his works: a bent, black-bottomed spoon stolen from a bar, and a syringe that he's used only a couple of times. He takes the packet of heroin out of his pocket and unfolds it carefully. This is the last of his stash, the emergency reserve he'd hidden safely away at his hotel. Enough for three reasonable fixes. But he's been clean for nearly a week. If he does it now, he won't want to stop again. Still, he wonders how he managed to stay clear of it for that long. A twisted experiment in self-control.

Well, now he's a little low on self-control.

He doesn't rush through the preparation. By now it's a part of the ritual. He is sober and has had no caffeine so his hands do not shake. He taps some heroin into the spoon. He draws about twenty cc's of water into the syringe from a glass by the sink. He squirts the water into the spoon, starting at the edges and spiraling it down into the powder. He squeezes a few drops of lemon into the mix. He stirs it briefly with the plastic end of the syringe. He cooks it until it simmers. He then tears a piece of filter from a cigarette and drops it into the spoon. He slides the needle into the filter and draws the solution into the syringe. Then he sets the syringe down on the sink. He rolls up his left sleeve, looking at his veins. He selects the vein on the side of his wrist. Moth doesn't like using the obvious and avoids it, the susceptible crook of the arm. He picks up the syringe and taps an air bubble out of it. Then he prods the vein until it stands up at attention like a good cadet. He's pleased that he won't have to tie off. He slides the needle in at the proper angle. The vein rolls. His veins tend to do that, which is why Orazio sometimes calls him "*Ballerina,*" because his veins always dance away. Patiently he tries again. This time he feels the vein give. He pulls back on the plunger. A red cloud of blood blooms inside the barrel, and the words of Burroughs come to him as usual – *Shoot your way to freedom* – as he presses the plunger. As is his habit, he reboots, pure red blood flushing in and out of the plastic. Then he slides the needle out, pressing a finger against the puncture in his wrist.

He feels the solution crawl up his arm and through his chest, burning uncomfortably, too much acid from the juice. Then the heroin hits his heart and rushes through his body and brain, the sensation familiar and friendly; he closes his eyes for a moment to better savor it. He opens them, then clears away all evidence of what he's done.

On the terrace, he lights a cigarette, and contemplates the darkness, both inside and out. Everything is just fine.

FOUR

In the morning, Moth goes out to see the social worker. First, he has his wake-up fix and then makes himself a cup of tea in the solitude of the empty apartment. His niece is at school, the adults at work. He feels good. He gets dressed, brushes his teeth, and answers the phone when it rings: Luciano, wanting to know if he was going to make it to his appointment. Moth tells him that he was just on his way out the door. Luciano tells him to come back for lunch. Moth says it's no problem, then his brother hangs up. Moth would be annoyed about how controlling his brother is acting, but, in his current state of mind, it's hard to care too much about anything.

The social worker is a young woman who seems genuinely nice. Moth answers all the questions about his drug history, from the first time to his current use and all the other drugs in-between. The first time had been when he was twenty-four years old. It had been offered to him by an ex-boyfriend of his, whom he had run into by sheer chance one night in a bar. Moth hesitated and stalled for several hours until curiosity had gotten the better of him. He had done just about every other drug there was except heroin. He had heard about how great it was. He'd read several books by authors addicted: Burroughs, Huncke, DeQuincey, Algren – books which had revealed everything and nothing. He had also heard how dangerous it was. But the danger of it appealed greatly to Moth. He told himself the usual story: *I'll only try it once.*

The first time is permanently etched in Moth's memory. After a few hours at the bar, his ex suggested that they go somewhere else. It was summer, so they ended up walking to the park. His ex had already shot up and was looking quite relaxed, but totally lucid. Finally, his ex asked Moth if he had made a decision. Moth said yes. There was no one else in the park, and they were sitting on the grass in a secluded area among some trees. His ex took a syringe out of his pocket. Moth stared at it – to be honest, he hadn't considered using a needle. He'd imagined snorting it. But that was the choice presented to him: needle or nothing. His ex reassured him that the needle was clean, and that it was better than snorting, anyway, up the nose wouldn't have a decent effect. Moth was extremely nervous about being out in the open and about the dose. His ex also reassured him that the dose was extremely small, he wasn't going to risk an overdose, and, as for the place, there was no one here and it would only take a minute.

"Okay," Moth said.

"Roll up your sleeve," said his ex.

Moth rolled up his sleeve and offered his arm. His ex's fingers stroked the susceptible underside of Moth's arm with a surprisingly gentle and delicate touch. He made a remark about how good Moth's veins were, close to the surface of the skin, a perverse sort of compliment. Moth's eyes never left the needle.

"Hold still," his ex said, and slid the slender needle in.

Moth felt the uncomfortable prick and held his breath. His ex's every movement was slow and precise. There was something about the act which reminded Moth of sex: the stroking, the penetration, then the pleasure. He became aware that his ex was staring at his face as he pulled the needle out.

A moment passed. "Well?" said his ex.

Moth didn't feel anything at first. "Nothing," he said.

"It wasn't a big dose," his ex said apologetically.

Soon after, they rose to leave. They started walking back to the bar where Moth had left his car. It was during the walk that Moth became aware of a strange sensation in his body, particularly his head. He knows that he and his ex were talking the entire length of the walk, but he can't remember anything they actually said. At Moth's car, his ex gave him his new phone number before saying good night. At this point, Moth's stomach hurt. He climbed into the car and started driving home, but he had only driven a few blocks before he had to pull over and get out of the car. He puked on the sidewalk. It was the easiest vomit he'd ever had, not uncomfortable at all, and, afterwards, he felt so much better. He went home and smoked a cigarette on the balcony. His lover, Quentin, who hadn't given him the watch yet, but would in a few months on Moth's twenty-fifth birthday, was already asleep in the bedroom. Moth sat in the dark, analyzing the sensation. He felt like he'd just had a fabulous orgasm, relaxed, but that was it. He assumed that it was always like this, which he learned later that it wasn't, and he didn't really like it. It was partly due to this assumption that Moth did heroin again, honestly believing that he wasn't the type of person who became addicted.

The second time was an even worse experience than the first, but he isn't asked, and he doesn't offer to tell that story.

Instead, he tells the social worker about his current use, very on-again, off-again. Moth tends to go on binges, every day as much as he can, maybe fixing four times a day. And then he would stop for a while, up to a few months. Since being in Urbino, he's been using in what he considers to be moderation: twice a day, a relatively low dose. The social worker asks him if he'd like to go into a methadone treatment program. He declines. He's been on methadone before, and he hated the hassle of having to get up early and drag his sick self down to the clinic to wait for the dose, and then wait another half hour for the dose to work. Plus, methadone had no kick to it. It was too subtle.

They conclude the discussion and set another appointment for Thursday.

Outside, the day is glorious. The clouds have broken and now the sun is out. Moth wishes that he hadn't lost his sunglasses. For some reason, the light in Italy seems brighter than the light in America. People were always writing about the quality of light in Italy, and though it makes no sense that the sun would shine more brightly here, he now understands the sentiment.

On his way back to Luciano's, he walks through town. In the main square he sees Sam sitting on the steps and smoking, wearing John Lennon sunglasses and a long, black trench coat. Moth sits beside him and asks for a cigarette. Moth asks him what he's up to. Sam says,

"Nothing." Then asks Moth if he heard about what happened in Rats' Alley the other night. Moth tells him that he was there. "You're kidding," Sam says. Moth tells him about jail, about staying at his brother's, and about his meeting with the social worker. Sam is sympathetic.

Moth finds sympathy, particularly from another man, uncomfortable. He changes the subject. "Where's Orazio?"

"He's around," Sam says. "If you don't run into him later, come by the house tomorrow."

"Oh, yeah?" Moth says. "I heard from Juan that your brother went to Rimini."

"He went."

"How did that go?"

"He was successful," Sam reveals.

"I see," Moth says, then stands up. "I have to go."

"Wait a second," Sam says.

Moth watches as Sam opens his bag and rummages around inside it. Sam looks a lot like his brother, only with paler hair and a more innocent air, which may be due to his age: nineteen. His real name is Dante, but he is really interested in Buddhism, so he calls himself Samsara, after the Buddhist belief. *Samsara:* the cycle of perpetual death and rebirth of all unenlightened living beings, which is pervaded by suffering. A bit morbid, when Moth thinks about it. But Sam does have a morbid streak to him, dresses all in black, and knows about Bauhaus and Sisters of Mercy and Front 242 and Ministry.

"Orazio wanted you to have this." Sam hands him a flyer, an announcement for a poetry reading at eight o'clock tonight. "Pasolini," Sam adds.

Moth isn't crazy about Pasolini's poetry, but the man himself had led an interesting life - brutal murder by an underage male prostitute included. "Maybe I'll go," he says, but he doesn't recognize the place. "Where's it at?"

Sam explains where the reading will be held. Then: "Hey, *Farfalla-*" Sam says with a grin "-you didn't give me the question of the day."

Moth gives him the Marx question. If religion is the opiates of the masses, then what are opiates?

"The obvious would be to make that statement reciprocal," Sam says, "and say that opiates are religion."

Moth smiles. "Yes, but the religion of whom?"

"Not of the masses," Sam reasons. "Of the minority."

"In this case, who is the minority, if religion is of the majority?"

"Atheists." Sam thinks for a moment. "So your point is that opiates are the religion of atheists."

"Almost," Moth says. "Tell me, do you know any junkies who believe in God?"

"Orazio believes in God."

"Does he really believe, or does he just say he does?"

"Huh. Hard to say."

"I'll put it another way: Does Orazio worship God or does he worship the needle?"

Sam grunts in agreement. "So your point is: junk is a form of religion."

"It involves ritual, rites of passage, devotion, and ecstasy. Do you deny that?"

"I don't deny anything," Sam says. "It's not my place to deny."

In the evening, Moth goes to the poetry reading. He has to convince his brother to let him go, but it isn't too difficult. Poetry writing runs in the family. Luciano had even published a small chapbook of his own pennings a few years ago that didn't do much as far as being successful. There had even been a poem in the chapbook about Moth, less than flattering, but still well-constructed, solid.

Moth, too, has published some poems in a few small literary magazines. He had been encouraged by his lover, Quentin, the man who had given him the watch. Another sensitive soul, he, too, had written poetry. Moth remembers the late nights in which Quentin sat at the desk in a circle of soft light, a long finger pressed against his lips tense with birthing words. The same look as when he would grade the compositions of his students about Rimbaud or Apollinaire. He taught French literature at a private school in Boston, and he took it very seriously, as he took everything seriously. Moth, although he hadn't realized at the time, had won him over by quoting a line from Baudelaire on the night they met, in the original French. Moth had studied French in high school, and he remembered a good deal of what he had learned. For some reason, once a poem had entered his head, it stuck there permanently, the way song lyrics stayed in other people's heads.

Water under the bridge, as they say. Or rather: a bridge thoroughly burned.

He sits at the back of the room. He arrived a few minutes early, so now he watches the room fill up. Must be nothing better to do in Urbino on a Tuesday night. He is somewhat surprised to see the paralegal from his brother's office come in, accompanied by a white-haired lady somewhere in her sixties. Obviously the mother. They sit up near the front. Arturo looks around the room briefly, but doesn't notice Moth.

A few minutes later, some chapbooks are passed around, and a very old man sits down at the microphone up front. The old man starts talking about Pasolini and then this and then that. He talks for so long that Moth starts feeling restless, only half-listening. *Where's the poetry?* He flips through the chapbook. Besides Pasolini talking about his garden and his dead boy lover, there are also a few poems by Ungaretti. Moth reads.

"*E me ne stacco sempre*
straniero
Nascendo
tornando da epoche troppo
vissute."

And I always tear myself away / foreigner / being born / returning from times experienced too much.

There's something about that he likes. Meanwhile, the ancient man drones on. Moth casts a glance at Arturo. He looks bored, but Moth notes that at least he's too polite to resort to sneaking glances at his cell phone.

Finally, the moment of poetry arrives. The old man goes all out, melodramatic, roaring and rumbling and pausing too long at the pauses. *Where the hell did they get this guy?* Pasolini must be turning over in his grave at this disgusting display.

Afterwards, he walks past Arturo. This time Arturo notices him. Impulsively, Moth decides to stop. "*Ciao,*" Moth says.

Arturo looks at him suspiciously, but says, "*Ciao.*"

Arturo's mom fixes Moth with her fish-eyes in a pale and penetrating Scorpio stare. Moth realizes that this must be a hereditary trait. "Arturo," she says, "why don't you introduce me to your friend?"

Arturo thinks about saying that this guy is not a friend, but Moth is already introducing himself. "My name's Michael Gallo," he is saying.

"Luciano's little brother?" Arturo's mom asks.

"Yes, *Signora.*"

Moth sees by Arturo's expression that this is new news to him. Obviously Luciano doesn't like to brag about him.

"You're back in Urbino," she says and then turns to her son. "Why didn't you tell me?"

Incredibile, Arturo thinks. "Was I supposed to?"

"Why not?" his mom says. "Michael comes back after all these years. And you were such good friends. Don't you remember how angry you were when he left? You were so upset that you kicked the ball inside the house and broke a window."

Arturo mulls it over. She's right. He looks at Moth in this new perspective. But even if they had been friends when they were little boys, they weren't friends now. "I don't remember, Ma."

"Do you still play soccer?" she asks Moth.

"No, ma'am. Soccer's not very popular in America."

"That's right, America. Did you like it?"

Moth and Arturo's mother start conversing about America, and all about Moth's parents. Arturo feels himself growing agitated. Then he remembers an occasion in which he and Moth and two other boys had been playing soccer. Arturo had moved to kick the ball and had hit Moth in the mouth with his foot, and Moth had run home in tears. Arturo had felt bad at the time, but now he enjoys the memory.

"What are you smiling about?" his mother asks him.

"Nothing. I was just thinking about the time that I kicked Michael in the face."

Moth narrows his eyes at Arturo. *Bastard*. Then he smiles, touching his front tooth. "You knocked out one of my teeth," he recalls. "At least it wasn't a permanent tooth."

"At least," Arturo echoes, thinking to himself, *I'll be more than happy to knock out another one if you try to provoke me.*

"You like poetry?" Mom asks Moth.

"I write some."

"What did you think of the reading?"

"Well," Moth says, "there's always the hope that in fifty years after I'm dead, a bunch of people who didn't give a shit about me in this life will sit around and listen to some dry, withered-up, erudite coot read my poetry badly."

Arturo sighs and rubs at his forehead, but his mother just fixes Moth with that cool, penetrating stare and says, "Twenty years have passed and you haven't changed. You're still the same."

Arturo takes her by the arm. "It's getting late, Ma, let's go."

~

He has two choices. It always comes down to this, a fork in the road. As far as Moth can tell, he's always at the same fork. He knows that it's a grand oversimplification to view his choices this way, as either black or white, but life is full of oversimplification, and it is human nature to split up and categorize and organize and label. Pro versus con. Day versus night. Male versus female. Heaven versus Hell. Good versus bad. Forget dubious, forget dusk and dawn, forget hermaphrodite, non-binary, and bisexual. Forget purgatory. But good or bad, these are Moth's choices.

He could go back to Luciano's house, what he's promised to do, and be good. Or he could go to The Dive in hopes of finding Orazio since he knows Orazio's holding and be bad.

Really, there is no choice.

He walks toward The Dive. If it is cold outside, he doesn't feel it. The last fix he took before the poetry reading warms him from the veins out. He looks at his watch, although he knows that it's just after 9:30. He slows his pace, realizing it's too early. The Dive won't be open yet. Coming into the main square, he looks at the people. No one he knows. He decides to duck into a small, crowded bar to his right to waste some time.

He has three thousand lire and some change to his name so squeezes his way up to the bar and asks the price of a glass of house wine. The girl behind the bar tells him two thousand. He asks for a glass of red. He lights a cigarette while waiting. She places the glass in front of him, and Moth lays his last two thousand lire bill on the bar, but she doesn't seem to notice it. Moth raises his eyes to the girl's face and sees that she's not even looking at him; she's looking at something over his left shoulder. Moth hesitates a moment, his mind slow and honey-thick, then wonders what the hell she's looking at with such intensity. He turns his head slowly, as if he's moving through syrup, and casts a glance over his shoulder. His eyes come in direct contact with the gold eyes of the Stranger, who is standing behind Moth so close they are almost touching.

Moth jumps. The smile. The same reaction, even though it shouldn't be possible. "You…" Moth murmurs.

Those gold eyes sweep over Moth's face. "How's your 'nothing'?" the Stranger says, his tone too familiar, teasing.

Moth, his high still strong, finds his thoughts roll recklessly of his mouth. "Right now it's really something."

"Oh, really?" the Stranger says.

"Really," Moth says, turning toward him.

The Stranger tilts his head, studying Moth. His smile, like Moth's erection, grows. Moth doesn't understand the connection between the

Stranger's mouth and his dick, but he would very much like there to be one.

"We have to stop meeting like this," the Stranger says.

"It seems to me," Moth responds, "that we haven't actually met."

"Words, just words." The Stranger places a hand on Moth's shoulder. "Come with me."

Moth does not need to be asked twice. He follows the Stranger out of the bar.

They cross the square. "Do you live around here?" the Stranger asks.

"I live with my brother."

"Ah," the Stranger says. They turn up Via Rafaello. "Have you ever fucked in a park?"

Moth almost stops walking from the shock. "Excuse me?"

The Stranger casts him a mischievous glance, openly sexual. "I asked you if you'd ever fucked in a park."

"I, uh…" Moth stammers. "Yeah."

"Good," says the Stranger.

Moth's mind reeling, they walk a few paces up the hill in silence. He can't seem to organize his thoughts. Then, "So, do you have a name?"

The Stranger looks straight up the road before them. "Of course I have a name."

Moth waits, expecting more, but there isn't any. "Well, aren't you going to tell me what it is?"

"No," the Stranger says.

"Don't you want to know mine?"

The Stranger looks at Moth again. "Words, just words."

Moth hums to himself. The beautiful ones are always the most difficult. "I happen to like words."

"Ah, yes," the Stranger drawls. "A writer, are you? A poet?"

"A poet," Moth admits.

"Well," the Stranger says slowly. "It's not your poetry that I'm interested in."

"Really?" Moth says. He can't think of what else to say.

At the top of the hill, they turn left and walk into the park. In the distance, Moth spies some people sitting on one of the benches, a group of young men drinking bottles of beer. "We're not alone."

The Stranger stops and turns to face Moth. "Do you want to change your mind?"

"I don't know," Moth starts to say and then the Stranger touches him.

Something happens to Moth when the Stranger touches him. He feels the light touch, the gentle hand on his bare neck, then a sensation of warmth creeping through his body, a warmth which turns into something else – sexual excitement, tension, a full-body throb, a choking desire. Moth goes blind, feels himself on the border of an orgasm, like nothing he's ever felt before. The Stranger drops his hand and Moth floats out of the sensation, staring at the Stranger in awe and confusion.

"Come on."

Around the corner, the Stranger pushes Moth against the shadowed wall of the old fortress. His gold eyes shimmer in the dim lunar light. His hands bold. Again the sensation, new, but oddly familiar. Moth locks his hands around the Stranger's neck, under the thick, black curtain of hair. His head swims; his heart races then slows as he stops breathing, the hands on his chest, under his shirt. His body explodes in a sudden and violent orgasm which offers no release. Tremors of pleasure tear through Moth, who would collapse to the ground if it weren't for the wall behind him and the arms of the Stranger keeping him on his feet. Moth is out of his head, engulfed in the sensation as it intensifies, only vaguely aware of the Stranger's pale hands on Moth's belt, and then ---

A blur of movement, an angry staccato of multiple voices, Moth collapses on the ground, only to be jerked roughly to his feet again, the moon in his eye, a pale burst of firework pain in his gut and then falling, falling, dirt in his mouth, incomprehensible shouting, his body mute and failing as he tries to focus his vision, sees a wave of black hair thrown against the moon, the grotesque shapes of men, the echo of breaking glass, then slow, as if underwater, someone strikes, a fountain of blood jets upward as a body arcs back, and he tastes his fear, legs useless and numb; the dark shapes scatter like roaches in a bright light, a cacophony of crickets drowned out by the cold blue wail of a siren.

FIVE

The wail of the door buzzer. A static crackle. A thin voice moving along a wire. "*Chi è?*"

"*Michele.*"

The front door clicks open. Moth climbs up the stairs to where Sam is waiting at the apartment's door, already dressed: black pants, black boots, torn black sweater about three sizes too big for him. "Hey, *Farfalla*," Sam says, letting him in. Sam closes the door, catching a glimpse of Moth's face. "What happened to you?"

"Orazio?" Moth asks.

"Still asleep," Sam says, but he is already moving to the door on the right, the one bedroom where Orazio sleeps. He opens the door without knocking, calls to his brother. Orazio mumbles something incomprehensible, then Sam gestures Moth over.

Orazio is sitting up in his bed, a large mattress on the floor of a small room, amid a jumble of blankets and pillows. The white walls are bare except for a crucifix over the bed and a few photos haphazardly taped to the walls. On one side of the room, a long, low table is stacked with schoolbooks and a cassette player. It's a room without windows. On the other side of the room, there's a dresser with a mirror above it.

Orazio turns on a small study lamp on the floor by the bed. His face is still puffy with sleep. He tells Moth to come in. Moth enters and sits at the edge of the bed. Orazio, in t-shirt and boxers, gets out of bed and walks barefoot, on the balls of his feet, to the bathroom.

Sam offers Moth a cup of tea. Moth asks if there's any coffee. Sam says there is, then goes to fix a cup. Orazio comes back to the bed, rubbing at his eyes, lights a cigarette. He looks at Moth for a moment with narrowed eyes. When he speaks, his voice is like the slash of a razor. "What happened to you?"

Moth makes a vague gesture.

Orazio's eyes flicker over Moth's face, assessing, suspicious, vaguely angry. "Sam told me what you said about the other night," he says.

"What happened? Did you lose your mind? What the fuck were you thinking walking around with the stuff on you?"

What Moth had been thinking at that point doesn't seem worth discussing. "I'm tapped out. It's finished."

"You didn't tell the cops anything, did you?"

Moth shoots Orazio an indignant look. *Just like Orazio to think of himself above all else.* "You think I would?"

Orazio leans back against the wall as the edge in his gaze softens. "No. Forget it."

Moth glances at his watch. "Listen. I really can't stay long. I'm supposed to be at my brother's office right now."

Orazio shrugs. "Yeah, okay. I know. Do you want for now, or for later?"

"Both."

Orazio gets up and goes to the table. He opens the drawer and takes out a small bag. "You have money?"

Moth shakes his head. "How about a loan?"

Orazio sighs. "Can't do it. I can fix you now, but I can't give you anything to take away. Rent's due in a couple of days."

"Then fix me now. I can't face my brother like this."

"Okay," Orazio says, pulling out his gear. "Sam, it's time!" he calls.

"Coming!" Sam calls back.

Orazio fingers the bag absentmindedly, looking at Moth. "Unless–"

"Unless what?"

"We could do a trade."

Moth eyes his friend suspiciously. "What do you want?"

Orazio makes a gesture, a tap of his finger against his wrist.

They're both aware that this is a turning point in their relationship, the fact that Orazio is cold enough to have the nerve to ask for the watch.

Moth stares at the Movado, his only possession of value. He thinks about the man who gave it to him. He remembers one time when Quentin had made love to him – not sex, but *love, love, love,* kisses and movements languid and gentle, and the experience had been so beautiful that Moth had actually cried.

Other than the memories that haunt him, it's the only thing he has left of that relationship. Moth unstraps the watch and hands it to Orazio.

Sam comes in, handing Orazio a glass of water, a spoon, and a lemon half. Orazio starts to prepare the solution. He asks Sam to find some syringes. Sam rummages through the drawer. *This one's new. Give it here. Turn on the light.*

Moth gets up and turns on the overhead light. Orazio holds the needle against the light. *Yeah, it's new. That's for Moth. Here's mine. Mark that one. Where's the knife. Right there.*

A throaty gurgle comes from the kitchen: the espresso maker. Sam excuses himself. He returns a few moments later and passes a cup to Moth, squatting down beside him, peering curiously into Moth's face. "Did you get into a fight?"

Moth reaches up and touches the scratch by his left eye. "More or less."

"More or less," Orazio repeats, amused. "Hand me that belt."

Moth watches Orazio, standing before the mirror, the belt taut, searching. A moment. The clatter of the buckle as it hits the floor. Sam hands him a cigarette. Orazio hands him a syringe. He picks up the other, looking at Moth strangely. "I'm going to do you myself," he says.

Sam cocks his head. He can feel the strange tension in the air. "I don't think that this is appropriate for my young eyes," he says, and leaves the room.

Orazio sits down across from Moth, the cigarette dangling from his mouth, and takes Moth's arm in his deft hands. "Tell me."

Moth talks. He tells Orazio how he went to the poetry reading last night, then to the bar where he saw the Stranger. He tells Orazio that they went to the park. He doesn't tell Orazio about the sensation he felt when the Stranger touched his neck. He doesn't tell Orazio about how he came in his jeans, cock still locked in. And then–

"Wait," Orazio says and floods him with relief.

Moth falls back on the bed, sighing. He closes his eyes. Opens them. Drinks the shot of espresso and lights a cigarette.

"And then–?" Orazio asks.

"A couple of guys jumped us before anything happened," Moth says. "Then the police showed up."

Moth doesn't describe his night, another night at the station-- though this time as a witness, not a criminal, despite that they had made him feel like one. Moth's testimony had been close to useless. He couldn't remember much, insisting that the whole thing had been a big blur, which was the truth.

They'd picked up one of the other guys who had jumped them, whose story collaborated with Moth's story, that Moth hadn't really done anything, it had been the other who had cut the boy with a broken bottle. The interrogation. *Who was the culprit? What is his name?* Moth didn't know. They didn't believe him. *What were you doing with him, why did you go with him to the park?*

"What happened to him?" Orazio asks.

"Took off." Moth sits up. "I have to take off, too."

Orazio gets up and fixes a bag for Moth. Moth slips it into the inner pocket of his coat. Moth stands up, putting his coat on. "Who is he, anyway, this boyfriend of yours?"

"I was hoping you could tell me," Moth says, then describes him.

Orazio makes a vague gesture. "Never seen him. He's not from Urbino."

"I already knew that."

Orazio accompanies Moth to the door. At the door, Moth says, "Hey, Sam, I've got a question just for you."

On his mattress in the corner of the room against the window draped with a painted cloth of Ganesha, the elephant god, Sam looks up from his sketchbook. "Oh, yeah? Go on."

"You know Rousseau? He said that man is born free, but everywhere he is in chains. But what if the man really likes being in chains? Does that mean he's really free?"

Sam smiles. "I like that."

Orazio scowls at Moth. "I wish you wouldn't put ideas like that in his head," he admonishes. "He's perverse enough as it is. I mean, what would our poor mother say if she knew?"

Already tired of studying, Arturo closes the book he was reading, and slides it over to join the other books in the large pile on one corner of the desk. He picks up the phone when it rings. A call for Gabriele Fiesta, who is out of the office at the moment, having gone to Pesaro. Arturo takes a message. He hangs up and reaches for the case file on his desk that he's been meaning to read. The phone rings again. This time, it's his girlfriend Chiara. She tells him that her brother called because her mother slipped on the stairs this morning and badly sprained an ankle. Arturo asks her if she's going to see her mother. She tells Arturo that he's read her mind again. She says that she'll drive up to Ravenna this afternoon, then drive back after dinner, so she won't see him until much later this evening. Arturo tells her to be careful and that he loves her and they hang up.

Murder leaps out at him when he opens the file. A man who killed his wife. Unfortunately, there was nothing unusual about that. This murderer, however, ended up not in prison but in a psychiatric hospital. He'd given some very unusual testimony. He'd become convinced that his wife's body had been taken over by aliens. He was afraid for his life, positive that his wife, now an alien, wanted to kill him. He claimed that she oozed poison out of her pores, that she intended to use her "venomous embrace" to make him her victim and then devour him. Lethal sex and cannibalism. Stuff from a horror film.

The door of the office opens, and Moth steps in. "*Ciao*," Moth says and sits down in one of the chairs across from Arturo.

Arturo moves his hand to the intercom. "I'll tell Luciano that you're here."

"No," Moth says. "Don't."

Arturo gives him a quizzical look, but honors the request by withdrawing his hand from the intercom. He watches Moth, who takes a pack of Marlboros out of his pocket. Moth shakes loose a cigarette and puts it in his mouth. He then looks at Arturo, and holds the pack out to him. Arturo waves away the offer.

Moth leans back in his chair. "I hope I didn't say anything to offend your mother last night."

Arturo hesitates a moment before he admits, "No, she found you rather charming, in an eccentric sort of way."

Moth seems to brighten. "Did she really say charming?"

Arturo makes a vague gesture.

Moth lazily scratches the back of his neck with his free hand. "Your mother has quite a penetrating stare," he comments. "I bet she sees everything."

"My mother is a very perceptive woman," Arturo says.

Moth regards Arturo for a moment. "You don't have the same eyes, but you have the same stare."

Arturo makes a small half-hum, half-grunt instead of responding.

Moth leans forward to flick his cigarette over the ashtray on Arturo's desk, then leans back again. He notices that the Raphael print has been replaced by a cubism-inspired painting, most likely manufactured by Luciano's wife, who, Moth knows, has recently taken up abstract painting as a hobby. "Did she really say charming?" he asks again.

Arturo fingers the file on his desk. "Is your brother expecting you?"

Moth stares at his cigarette for a moment, as if the answer he is seeking can be found in the shifting smoke. "Yeah, but he doesn't want to see me."

Arturo makes the grunting-hum again. It's none of his business, so he doesn't ask. He looks down at the file. *The lunatic* husband knew his wife was *an alien* because he saw her go *through the change*. She was an alien *before* the change, but the change made her *more into an alien*.

"What are you reading?" Moth asks.

"A case."

"What kind of case?"

"A man who murdered his wife case."

Moth scratches his shoulder, under his jacket. "Not something that I'll ever do."

Arturo finds that comment rather strange. "Really?"

"Why'd he kill his wife?"

Arturo doesn't want to get into this. "He says that she changed."

Moth puts out his cigarette. "Tell me. What are your views on change?"

"Change?"

Moth nods.

"Change is good," Arturo says. "Change is necessary. If everything remained static, it would be like death."

Moth scrutinizes him. "How long have you lived in Urbino?"

"All my life."

"Hmm," Moth says.

The intercom buzzes and Luciano's voice crackles into the room. "Has Michael arrived yet?"

"He's here," Arturo says.

"Send him in."

~

Moth braces himself to face his brother by drawing in a deep, calming breath before turning the knob. But nothing could have prepared him for what happens next. He enters the room. His eyes fall on Luciano who is standing in front of his desk instead of sitting behind it like Moth expected. He meets his brother's eyes, accidentally. Luciano sees Moth's eyes, pinned within the false bright blue of his contact lenses. Something dark and furious passes over Luciano's face, a warning flicker. Moth catches the change as it flashes across his brother's expression, but, when Moth tries to bolt back through the door, he doesn't elude the grasp of Luciano's fist.

Moth's jacket is hooked in his brother's fingers. He hears the slap of his brother's hand against his face before he feels it. Moth struggles, lashing out. "Get your fucking hands off me," he growls.

"Where is it?" Luciano demands, face flushed. "Where are the fucking drugs?"

Moth lashes out again, hitting his brother ineffectually. "I said get your fucking hands off me!"

Luciano swings again, this time with his fist. At the same time, Moth slips free. The impact sends Moth back against the wall, dislodging a framed poster, which crashes to the floor, glass scattering. Then Luciano is on top of Moth, rifling through Moth's pockets. Moth struggles again and receives another slap. Luciano backs off. Moth's heart sinks down into his stomach when he sees the bag in Luciano's hand.

Arturo appears in the open doorway. He had just finished reading his file when he heard the crash. "Is everything okay?" he asks, hesitantly.

Luciano smooths back his hair, trying to compose himself. He puts the heroin in the filing cabinet and then locks it. "Everything's fine," Luciano says, voice an unsteady staccato. "Arturo, why don't you take a break at the bar."

It's more of a command than a question. Arturo goes.

Moth touches his mouth, his fingers slick with blood. He wipes his hand angrily on his jeans. He doesn't get up from the floor.

Luciano stares down at him. "I don't know what to do with you anymore."

Moth glares up at him. "You don't know, so – what? You beat me?"

"Maybe that's what you need."

Moth stares at the filing cabinet, feeling a flicker of panic "You're not my father. You can't tell me what to do."

Luciano lets this pass. "This is serious, Michael. A boy is dead."

This sinks into Moth's mind. He didn't know that the guy had died. "They attacked *us*," Moth says. "It was self-defense." He looks back up at his brother, who doesn't seem convinced. "I didn't kill anyone, so stop looking at me like I did."

Luciano sighs. "No, you're right. The only one you're responsible for killing is yourself." Moth glares at him, touching his mouth again, already swelling. "Maybe that's your business. Maybe I should let you."

"I didn't realize that I needed your permission to live or die," Moth says coldly.

Luciano stares for a long moment at his brother. Life has been a struggle for Moth for some time now. Before that, things seemed to have been going well. He'd been living in Boston with that high school teacher, publishing poetry and working steadily as a typesetter and later as a graphic designer for a well-known publishing company. Their mother had sent occasional letters to Luciano, and she'd never failed to give him all the details about his little brother. They had even met this high school teacher, Quentin. She had said that he was "a nice enough fellow," which really meant that he was wonderful.

Luciano heaves another sigh. "If you didn't look just like her, I'd swear you'd been adopted."

Moth makes a noise of disgust. He's heard this a thousand times already.

"Michael," Luciano says. "You have to tell the police about the man you were with last night."

"I told them everything I know."

"So, what you're saying is, is that you went to the park to have some sort of sexual escapade with a perfect stranger."

Moth lifts himself up off the floor. "This is bullshit."

"What do you mean by 'bullshit'?" Luciano asks.

"If you don't approve of me, of what I do, I don't even care."

Luciano shakes his head. "I don't approve of what you do. How can I? You're not stupid, Michael, you are aware of the risks surrounding your behavior. I mean using drugs. I don't mean you, who you are. I don't disapprove of your being gay, if that's what you think. You're right, I'm not father."

This remark strikes Moth in the heart. He turns his face away from his brother. "That's enough," Moth says quietly.

"You're right, that is enough," Luciano says. "I've had enough. Get out."

Surprised, Moth looks at his brother.

"You heard me," Luciano says. "I'm tired of you treating me like I'm the enemy. You don't appreciate your family. You don't appreciate shit. I don't want to see you if you're going to behave like a child. And I will not, under any circumstances, having you shooting yourself full of heroin in the house with my daughter there. So get out of my sight before I lose control of myself again."

Moth feels his throat constricting. Something is breaking somewhere.

No watch, no heroin, no brother, nothing, nowhere, no one. "Fine," Moth says, shards of broken glass grinding under his boot as he turns to go.

~

It is late. Night has fallen. Arturo sits at Fiesta's desk, in the back of the law office. He is alone. On the desk before him are three things: the file about the man who killed his wife, the file about the serial killer, and today's newspaper, all open, filling the space. The newspaper is open to the local *cronaca*. Of interest to Arturo is the article about a local boy who was killed in a fight last night by an unidentified assailant. Of more interest is the description of the assailant given by the witnesses. A man with long black hair and gold eyes.

In the file about the man who killed his wife because she changed into an alien is the claim that, when she changed, her eyes, once brown, had become golden.

As for the serial killer, he was described as a man with dark hair and yellow eyes, although in his documents he was listed as having green eyes.

Arturo is aware that all this could be a folly. However, the folly has hooked him.

After work he'd gone home for lunch. In the empty apartment he'd watched the news with last night's leftover pasta. Without Chiara, he felt restless. He was used to her presence. Maybe for this reason he went out in the evening. He ran into a friend of his in town. They chatted for a while at the bar over an aperitif. Then Arturo stopped for pizza. At the pizza place, he browsed the newspaper. The article caught his eye, at least for the fact that it was rare that anyone was murdered in Urbino, and also out of the morbid curiosity to discover if the dead boy was anyone he knew. The article became more interesting as he read. There was a heavy implication of what the boys had been doing up by the fortress before the fight ensued. This doesn't interest Arturo in the slightest. In fact, homosexuality makes him uncomfortable, for he finds it unnatural, and difficult to fathom. But he doesn't condone what the instigators did, resorting to violence against the gays. *Live and let live,* Arturo thinks.

What interested Arturo was the killers with gold eyes connection. So Arturo took the newspaper, stopped at his apartment for the serial killer's file, and returned to the law office. He let himself in with his key. He then spread out his papers on Fiesta's desk, leaving the front office dark so as not to be disturbed.

Now he passes some time, rifling through other files, looking for similar connections, other killers with golden eyes. It grows later, darker. He feels the strain in his back from crouching over the filing cabinet. He closes the filing cabinet, stands up, and stretches his whole body toward the ceiling. And then, while his arms are still above his head, a noise breaks into the silence.

Arturo freezes, listening. Again, the rattle of metal. The noise is coming from somewhere in the office. His heart quickens. It could be one of the lawyers having returned to pick up some forgotten paperwork. But he doubts it. Arturo glances around the office, looking for some sort of weapon with which to defend himself. There is nothing. He decides to go take a look anyway. Arturo once studied martial arts, so he is confident that he can defend himself if necessary. He steps out of Fiesta's office, treading lightly.

The light in Luciano's office has been switched on. Arturo looks in and sees Moth fiddling with the lock in Luciano's filing cabinet. "Hey!" Arturo snaps.

Moth startles, then relaxes slightly when he sees Arturo. "Christ, you scared me," Moth says. "What are you doing here?"

Arturo shoots him a look of disbelief. "What am I doing here? I work here. What the hell are you doing here?"

"A little B and E," Moth says in English.

"What?"

"Did you call the police?"

Arturo hesitates a moment, enjoying Moth's anxiety. "No."

"Are you going to?"

Arturo knows he should, but he has his reasons not to. "No."

Moth relaxes a little, his shoulders slumping. "In that case, do you have a key to this?"

"No," Arturo says, although he wouldn't give it to him even if he had.

"Okay," Moth says. He pulls a metal bar out of the back of his jeans and wedges it into the top of the filing cabinet. He takes the bar in both hands and yanks it. Arturo winces at the sound of the metal drawer as it rips loose. Moth puts the bar back under his coat and reaches into the drawer to take what's his.

"*Madonna*," Arturo murmurs, disgusted. "Your brother will know it was you."

Moth straightens up. "That doesn't concern me."

He starts walking out. Arturo sidesteps to let him. Except...

"Wait," Arturo says.

Moth stops in the doorway in front of Arturo. They are the same height, eye to eye. He waits.

"I want to talk to you."

Moth takes a hard look at Arturo. Arturo's expression is neutral, giving away nothing. Moth glances back into his brother's office. The broken 18th century pastoral picture is still there, propped against the wall, but the broken glass has been swept up. Moth wonders if Arturo was the one who cleaned it up. Moth's hand flutters to the light switch, flicking it off. He turns back to Arturo, who is more handsome in the dim light of the hall, flushed with shadow. "What for?"

"I want to talk to you about last night," Arturo says.

"Why?"

"I have some information which might interest you."

Moth finds himself intrigued. He doesn't know if he is more intrigued by the man or by the information. "All right then. But not here."

"We can go to my house," Arturo says. Having Moth in his house is less disagreeable to him than being seen in public with him. He can already imagine the backlash it would cause if he were to be seen in the company of a drug-using homosexual at a bar or something.

Moth nods. The junk is burning a hole in his pocket, but he feels all right, it can wait. "You live near here?"

"Yeah," Arturo says. "Come on."

~

Arturo unlocks the door and lets Moth into the apartment. Moth slowly peels off his coat as he looks around. By the front door, there is a small, narrow bathroom. They are in a living room, which branches off to an open air kitchen to the left, too small to hold a kitchen table. To the right, in a corner, is a cheap desk in chaos, reminding Moth of his college days. Across from the desk is the bedroom door, closed. In front of him is a comfortable armchair and a small sofa, next to a very small end table made of the same cheap material as the desk. Behind him is a TV propped up on a crate. On the walls are some abstract sketches of women reminiscent of Miró. Moth imagines that the sketches are not Arturo's; he doesn't strike Moth as the artistic type. Arturo takes Moth's coat.

"Can I smoke?" Moth asks, feeling very American for asking.

Arturo shrugs. He lays Moth's coat on the counter that separates the kitchen from the living room, adding his own coat to create a pile. He goes into the kitchen and finds an ashtray. He comes back and tells Moth to sit down. Moth puts himself on the sofa. Arturo, not surprisingly, takes the chair. Moth lights a cigarette, wondering if Arturo is aware of his sexual orientation.

Moth tends to keep that private. He doesn't flaunt it like some men. His lover, Quentin, had remarked once that it was indeed obvious by Moth's eyes, by how he looked at other men. Then there was the cigarette thing. Moth held his cigarette in a feminine manner, between his index and middle fingers, hand aloft, wrist bent back with a flair, or forward, limp, like a stereotype. Moth thinks that he has beautiful hands and he takes care of them, the nails slightly long and buffed, using a cream of beeswax and honey to keep the skin soft. Eyes and hands. He looks at Arturo's hands as they flip through one of the files he brought home with him.

Arturo hands Moth the file about the man who killed his wife. He leans forward, closer to Moth, to point out a particular passage. Moth picks up his scent: soap, a particular brand of Italian deodorant which Moth also uses called Infasil, no aftershave. Arturo, with his clean soap scent and long eyelashes: a paragon of the boy next door. "Read this," Arturo says, then leans back again.

Stop it, Michael, Moth tells himself, even though he's aware that he's already developed a crush. Not the first time he's had a crush on a straight man. Of course, he'd lost a lot of sleep over that. Moth averts his eyes to read.

Arturo watches Moth for a reaction. At this point, he feels no particular aversion to his guest. He feels indifferent. His eye falls on Moth's mouth, which is slightly swollen from where Luciano hit him, and Arturo almost feels sorry for him. Almost.

Moth stops reading, thinking. "Very strange," he says.

Arturo gives him the other file about the serial killer to look at. Moth reads. Then he stubs out his cigarette, looking at Arturo. Arturo is sitting at the edge of his chair, waiting for Moth's reaction, his expression serious.

"Your interest in this… is what?" Moth asks.

"Nothing in particular," Arturo says. "Just an interest."

"You think there's a connection between this," Moth says, touching the files, "and–" Moth doesn't know what to call the stranger, "–what happened last night."

"The guy with gold eyes," Arturo clarifies. "What do you think?"

"What? That maybe he was an alien?"

Arturo shrugs. "I wouldn't go that far," he says. "But…"

"What?"

"Don't you find it unusual, this business about the gold eyes?"

Moth can see Arturo's mind moving quickly and decisively. Maybe not entirely off the mark, as Moth did indeed find it unusual. Feeling like the devil's advocate, Moth says, "Contact lenses."

"What?"

"The guy with the gold eyes," Moth explains. "He might have been wearing contact lenses. They have all colors now. Even lenses with smiley faces on them, you know?"

"It's possible. Do you believe it?"

"As opposed to what?"

"He is a killer," Arturo says, his tone suggestive.

"That was self-defense," Moth says. "Which seems rather different from what you've got: a serial killer who does only women with a hot shot, and a psycho who didn't want to fuck his wife."

Arturo is unmoved by Moth's vulgarity. "Sex, death, and eye color."

Moth startles. "What?"

"I'm doing research on sex crimes," Arturo explains. "And these are crimes involving sex."

Moth pauses. Then: "Why did you want to talk to me?"

Arturo senses Moth's discomfort. *Maybe the guy's ashamed of himself.* "Did you see today's paper?"

"No. Why?"

Arturo pulls out the paper, still open to the article. He watches Moth go pale as he reads it. Moth glances back at Arturo. *Okay, Arturo knows.* This bothers Moth for some reason, not only that Arturo knows about Moth's sexual orientation, but also that Moth is slut enough to go off with some stranger to be intimate in a dark shadow. Still, there's nothing judgmental about Arturo's expression, just intensity of interest.

"Okay?" Arturo asks.

"Okay, what?" Moth counters.

"Nothing," Arturo says. "I'm just saying that sex was involved."

"Sex is always involved."

"What do you mean?"

"I mean that if there's a man involved, then there's a ninety-nine percent chance that there's sex involved. Don't tell me that you don't think about sex about a hundred times a day."

A crinkle appears in Arturo's brow. "And, so?"

"I'm just saying that sex is always involved. Take any crime you like, there was probably sex in there somewhere. Sex is the biggest motivator."

"So," Arturo says, "if a guy robs a bank, sex is involved?"

"Sure," Moth says. "He needs the money to get sex. You know that nothing turns a woman on as much as a man with a lot of money."

"Not all women." Arturo says, thinking particularly of Chiara, who loved him even though he was broke. And then, "What do *you* know about women?"

Moth reaches for another cigarette. "I know more than I need to know."

Arturo looks at Moth with a serious intensity. It's almost too much for Moth to bear. He likes Arturo, a little too much, so serious and beautiful and soap clean. "Oh, yeah?" Arturo asks. "And what does that mean?"

"It means what you think it means," Moth says slowly.

"You've had sex with women?"

"Yeah," Moth admits.

Arturo feels a little respect for his guest for this fact. The first thing this loser has said that he could even remotely relate to. "Several?"

Moth did it, so he doesn't mind talking about it much, although it is due more to the fact that Arturo seems genuinely curious in a nonjudgmental way, hanging onto Moth's every word. "Three," Moth says, then, "Well, technically, two."

"Really? And how was it?"

"Well, I imagine that you know."

"I mean, how was it for you?"

Moth thinks for a moment. "Strange."

"Strange how?"

"Just… strange," Moth says. "Different."

"Did you… enjoy it?"

"A little, I guess."

"You must have felt something, if you did it more than once," Arturo points out.

"It wasn't terrible," Moth says.

"And did you…" Arturo trails off unexpectedly.

"Have an orgasm?" Moth fills in.

"Yes."

"With the first one."

"But not the second?"

"No."

"Did they…?"

"Come?"

"Yes."

"The first one."

"While you were inside her?"

"Yeah," Moth says. Then adds, "It took a while. I wasn't… used to it. She made a lot of noise. I thought she was going to wake her parents up."

"How old were you?"

"Sixteen. Almost seventeen."

"And the girl?"

"The same."

"Hmm," Arturo says. "Did you know you were…" Arturo makes a gesture, vague.

"Gay?"

"Yes."

"You mean before I had sex with a girl."

"Yes."

"I knew."

"Then why did you?"

Moth shrugs. "Curiosity."

Arturo rubs at his jaw, considering the discussion. "Hmm."

Moth watches Arturo's hand moving languidly over his jaw, the gesture both innocent and sensual. It is too much to bear. "And you?"

Arturo raises an eyebrow. "And me what?"

Moth feels his throat constricted and thick with hope. "Have you… ever been with a man?"

"No," Arturo replies quickly.

"Have you ever thought about it?" Moth asks.

"No, it doesn't interest me."

"Did anyone ever make a pass at you?"

"No."

"What would you do if a man made a pass at you?" Moth asks.

"I don't know," Arturo says, thinking that he might hurt anyone who tried with him. "I never thought about it."

Moth's heart throbs wildly. He won't know if he doesn't try. This could be his only chance. Arturo hasn't said anything to discourage him.

Watching Arturo's serious face, those green eyes so casual, Moth leans forward slowly. He places his hand on Arturo's thigh, just above the knee.. "Curious?" Moth asks tentatively.

Arturo's eyes widen a bit when Moth touches him. It agitates and confuses him for a moment, and he doesn't know what to do. This sort of thing happens to women all the time, but it never happens to him. Part of him feels disgusted. Another part violent. But he doesn't like violence.

"Look, I live with someone," Arturo says, as calmly as possible. ""My girlfriend," he adds emphatically.

Moth immediately withdraws, the rejection a nasty stab in his heart. "Really?" he says, as if nothing had happened. "I took you for the type who would still be living with his mother."

Arturo's anger flashes. "What the fuck is that supposed to mean?"

"Oh, nothing," Moth says.

The rattle of the front door ends the conversation. Both men look up as Chiara enters. Arturo rises to greet her and takes the grocery bags from her hand. She sees Moth on the sofa. She strides across the room and stops before him, offering her hand. "Hi, I'm Chiara."

"Michael," he says, taking the hand.

"Luciano's brother," Arturo adds from the kitchen. He's told her a little bit about Moth, but always referred to him as "Luciano's brother."

"Really?" she says. "Arturo's talked about you quite a bit."

Moth looks up at her. She is being sincere. "Oh, has he?" Moth drawls. "That's surprising."

"Don't mind him if he acts a little touchy," she says. "He gets that way sometimes, but he doesn't mean it."

"Chiara," Arturo mutters, annoyed.

She watches him unpacking the groceries. "Just leave that. I'll do it." She walks back to the kitchen, calling over her shoulder. To Moth: "Would you like something to drink?"

"Michael was just leaving," Arturo says.

Moth stands up, goes to get his jacket. "Yeah, I should go."

Chiara's gaze flutters between the two men, one eyebrow slightly arched. "I wasn't interrupting anything, was I?"

Moth smiles, amused.

"No, nothing," Arturo says.

After leaving Arturo's house, Moth walks to the center of town. He goes down a hill. He goes up another hill. Urbino is like that. He walks slowly, in no hurry, so he still has breath when he reaches the main square. He sees Sam, Juan, and a young blonde girl sitting on the steps in front of the *farmacia*, now dark and closed. They greet him.

Sam introduces the girl to Moth, her name is Lisa, from Lecce. Lisa from Lecce – has a nice ring to it. Moth gives the boy a cigarette and comes directly to the point. "Would it be all right if I crashed at your house tonight?"

Sam shrugs, tapping his boots on the steps. "I don't mind," Sam says. "I don't think Mr. Control would mind." Mr. Control is what Sam calls Orazio when Orazio isn't around. "I guess that means yes, if you don't mind sleeping on the floor."

"Oh, hell," Moth says. "I'll just sleep with Orazio."

Sam and Juan exchange a knowing glance and start snickering. Then Juan bursts out in laughter. "Damn, I'd let you stay at my house, if I could," Juan says, still laughing. "You are kind of cute, now that I look at you."

The boys laugh harder at Moth's expense, caught up in it. Moth is not amused. "I think you know what I mean."

"Don't forget to leave a nice tip!" Juan gasps out, laughing harder.

"You bastards," Moth says. He waits until they calm down. "What are you all doing, anyway?"

"You're looking at it," Juan says. "Exciting, isn't it?"

"A thrill a minute," Sam adds.

Moth looks around the square. The night is warm, so there are quite a few people.

Sam reaches up, wrangling his pale frizzy hair into something resembling a ponytail. "Hey, *Farfalla*, did you go to that thing?"

"What thing?"

"That Pasolini thing."

"Oh, yeah," Moth says. He tells them about the old guy who did the reading, giving them a reasonable impression, and they laugh in appreciation, which causes Moth to feel better about himself.

Sam muses. "If I get like that, weird and old, I don't mean just *old,* but weird and old, somebody shoot me."

"Oh, shoot yourself, you lazy bastard," Juan jokes.

Sam responds by giving Juan the finger.

"No, thanks, I've had bigger," Juan says.

Sam pouts, unable to think up a snappy comeback.

Moth ponders the change in Juan's attitude that comes about whenever Moth sees him with Sam, as opposed to when he sees Juan alone, or how Juan had been at The Dive the other night. Reserved and cautious then. Now, another story. The Spaniard's dark eyes flash with life.

"Where's your friend, the guy I saw you with the other night?" Moth asks Juan.

"Who, Dominick?" Juan says. "He's not my friend. He's an asshole."

"Takes one to know one," Sam murmurs.

Juan eyes the boy. "You know, I'd put you over my knee and spank you, but you'd probably like it too much." He turns back to Moth. "What was I saying?"

"You were saying that you hang out with assholes," Moth says dryly.

"Oh God, yes," Juan says, sighing dramatically. "And they're all Italian assholes, of course. You know what the problem with Italian assholes is? They're just like Spanish assholes. You, Michael, are lucky. At least you got to spend your time with American assholes. I imagine that American assholes are different. A breed apart."

"It seems to me that you're implying that everyone's an asshole," Sam remarks.

"Not everyone is an asshole," Juan says. "You, my dear, are a lazy bastard."

"And you?" Sam asks.

"Me? I'm the biggest asshole there is," Juan says, half-joking but half-serious.

A moment of silence settles down around them.

Lisa pipes up. "Hey, what time is it?"

Without thinking, Moth looks at his wrist, which is naked. He feels naked. But his internal clock tells him that it can't be much past ten.

"Early," Juan says. "Would anyone like to go get a drink?"

"I would," says the Lisa.

"I'm broke," Moth says.

"I've got five thousand," Sam says. "Are you buying?"

"Yeah, I'm buying," Juan agrees. "Does everyone want to go?"

Sam agrees. Lisa puts her hand on Sam's arm, as if he were agreeing for her sake, because she wanted to go. Moth agrees, too, and they go.

～

At a dark, underground bar they take a table and Juan buys the drinks. The conversation moves quickly, broken up by friendly insults and laughter. Juan starts telling stories about his past. One about this crazy old guy who roamed the streets of Juan's hometown, exposing himself occasionally to passing women and generally being a nuisance. One time, taking the matter into his own hands, Juan and his friends borrowed a camera, then followed the exhibitionist and waited for him to expose himself. When it happened, Juan and his friends started snapping pictures, calling to the guy to pose like a fashion model. The guy ran off. It didn't stop him from exposing himself again, however.

At the end of the story, Sam asks, "Do you still have the pictures?"

"What? Hell, no," Juan says. "Are you kidding? There wasn't even any film in the camera."

This leads to a discussion about some of the crazy people in Urbino. Sam tells them about a guy who reputedly can give himself a blowjob, among other odd behaviors. Which leads to a heated discussion about whether any of the men at the table would do it to themselves if they were so agile. Juan insists that they are lying when they deny it. Then Juan apologizes to Lisa for the graphic content of the discussion, but she just shrugs, indifferent. Which leads to a discussion about oral sex, then sex. Juan does most of the talking. There was the time he had sex with a girl on the hood of her car, still hot from the engine, on the side of a back road. Then the time in an alley in full daylight with a man he'd just met in a hotel bar, who was supposed to be at the airport catching his flight home instead of dallying with Juan. With a girl on a pool table. With another girl in front of a fireplace with several people in the room watching.

"That's how we met," Sam adds. "The first time I saw Juan, he was making love to this girl at a friend's house."

Moth nods, lights a cigarette.

"You three are awfully quiet," Juan says.

Moth leans forward, playing with his empty glass. "Let me ask you something. How many people have you been with?"

"Women or men?"

"Both."

Juan calculates. "Over a hundred," he says frankly. "And, since you want to talk numbers, what about you?"

"I didn't say I wanted to talk numbers," Moth says. "I was just curious."

"Three," Sam says.

Everybody looks at him.

"What?" Sam says, suddenly sorry that he spoke.

Juan takes the last swig of his beer. "Nothing wrong with three. That's what I think. And nothing wrong with a hundred. We're all free."

"Not according to Rousseau," Sam says.

"Oh, man is born free but everywhere he is in chains," Juan says with nonchalance.

Moth is surprised and impressed.

"If you ask me, Rousseau is full of shit," Juan says. "We are free. The problem is that most people don't know it. They don't realize that they're free. And then they only make it worse. They build their lives in little spaces. They weigh themselves down with all kinds of obligations: work, money, family, whatever. With meaningless things. Cars, houses, Armani suits, whatever they've been brainwashed to want, stuff they don't need. And not just with material things. Even with love. They make love conditional, nobody gives it freely. They make it ugly, try to cram it into their little spaces which they've already constructed. But I don't buy into that. They put obstacles in their own path, and everybody makes the path they want."

Moth recognizes Juan's last sentence. Clearly he's not the only one at the table who reads too much. "Paul Bowles."

"*The Sheltering Sky*," Juan says.

"What about the law?" Sam asks.

"Oh, fuck the law," Juan says and they all laugh. "Really, have you seen some of these stupid laws that exist? In some place in America, there's a law that still exists that makes it illegal to bathe on any day except Saturday. Take a shower on Monday, you're breaking the law. I mean, come on." Juan pauses for a second, looking at everyone. "These are stupid laws made by stupid people who don't realize that they are free."

A moment of silence. Then Sam says most seriously, "That's fucking profound."

Something about how he said it causes them to laugh again.

"Yeah, too profound," Juan says. "Let's find a more shallow subject. Like Sam, for example."

"Oh, go to hell, Juan," Sam says and pouts again.

Soon after, the party breaks up. They walk Lisa over to the stop to catch the last bus to the *colleghi* where she lives. Juan hangs around long enough to tell a story about an Armani suit which was destroyed in a burning car, then heads home. Once the bus pulls out from the stop, Moth and Sam walk back to Sam's house. The house is dark, no one is home. Sam drops his bag on the floor and clicks on a light.

"Don't ask me where Orazio is," Sam says. "Get you something?"

"I wasn't going to ask," Moth says. He pulls the metal crowbar out from under his jacket which had been digging somewhat painfully into his body all night, setting it down on the floor by the bedroom door, and rubs his back.

Sam eyes the bar. "Oh, I guess you've already seen my brother." He goes into the kitchen. He calls to Moth. "There's still a beer. Want to share it?"

"Sure."

Sam returns with two mismatched glasses and a Moretti already uncapped, giving the taller glass to Moth. "Make yourself comfortable."

There is only the big mattress and the floor. They sit on the edge of the mattress and Sam pours the beer. "Maybe you should invest in some furniture," Moth suggests.

"There was some but we got rid of it."

"Oh, yeah? What for?"

"Aesthetic reasons."

"Good reason," says Moth.

"Also for religious reasons. You know, attachments."

"Attachments?"

"It's better not to have too many attachments. I mean, to be a Buddhist, you have to get rid of all your attachments. They'll only make you suffer. Even if they make you happy at first, in the end it's all suffering."

Moth can't find an argument against the idea. "I see," he says.

They drink. Sam takes a cigarette. "*Farfalla*," he says. "Question."

Can a man be rid of all his attachments? Is happiness a mental disease? Can the human heart be broken beyond repair? Does the soul exist? What is the meaning of life? Are we really how others see us? Is there any limit to evil? Is there intelligent life elsewhere in the universe? Can the self be defined? Is unconditional love actually possible, or is it all conditional? Are there any truths which are absolute? Does anything matter?

"Can it be personal?" Moth asks.

Sam shrugs. "Doesn't mean I'll answer it."

"Have you ever been with a man?"

"No," Sam says. "Why? Are you making a pass at me?"

"No, I'm not making a pass at you," Moth says. "But if a man made a pass at you, what would you do?"

Sam draws on his cigarette, contemplating. "Depends on the man."

"Really?" Moth says. "Depends on what, exactly?"

"If I found him attractive," Sam says. "If I trusted him. It would have to be with someone I really trusted."

"Like Juan?"

"I knew you were going to ask me that," Sam says. "But, no, definitely not Juan."

"Interesting."

"What?"

"That you'd go with a man."

"I'd do it for the experience."

"The experience?"

"Sure," Sam says. "To try it. You know, you should try everything once. And, if you like it, you should keep doing it. And you know what they say: we're all bisexual by nature."

"They say that, but it doesn't make it true."

"Maybe," Sam says.

They finish the beer, chat a little while longer, then Sam announces that he needs to sleep so he can make it to class in the morning. Moth goes into Orazio's room. He removes his shoes. The half-crushed lemon is still on the table, forgotten. He finds the syringe from this morning and sets up his fix. Fixed, he settles himself down on the bed with his cigarettes, notebook, and pen and begins to write.

Burning one cigarette after another, he writes. Usually he finds it difficult to write when he's high, due to the fact that he keeps nodding off behind the pen, but this time it's different. He's been seized by the muse. The pen flies across the paper, his handwriting growing ever more jagged with the fury of the words as they gush forth. It is practically divine. His pen skitters over the page, filling it with the phrases forming fast and hot and thick in his head, he stops to consider, to savor, and to judge what is to follow, then writes again. He is at the bottom of the page when he hears the door open.

Orazio has had a shitty evening. At first, he's annoyed to see Moth sitting in his bed. *What the hell.* "What are you doing?"

"Wait a minute," Moth says, terse, without looking up. "Almost finished."

Orazio blinks. He contemplates Moth's concentration. *Poetry.* Orazio sits down on the bed and lights a cigarette, watching Moth's clenched fingers crawling sideways like a crab over the little book.

Drawing in a slow drag, Orazio reconsiders the situation. He could tell Moth about his awful experience, if he wanted to. Moth would listen. These poetic types were always sensitive. Other than Moth, who would listen? Orazio is a little short on friends these days, for one reason or another. Either Orazio fucked them over, or they tried to fuck him over. Usually over junk. He thinks about how true it is that junkies don't have any friends. Not that he considers himself a junky, of course. Orazio believes that he has it all under control. Like Moth. Moth seems to have it under control. Somewhat.

Moth stops writing. He stares at the page for a moment. Then he puts the pen down, looking at Orazio. Orazio sees that his eyes, behind the green lenses, are pinned. "How's it going?" Moth says, tentatively.

"You got your stuff back?" Orazio asks, suspicious.

"Yeah. Don't worry."

Orazio takes out his cigarettes, even though he has one burning in the ashtray near his feet. "Just asking."

Moth watches Orazio playing with the pack, turning it over and over in his hands. A moment passes. "What's wrong?" he asks.

"Have you ever..." Orazio starts, then censors himself.

"Have I ever what?"

Orazio stares at the cigarette pack. "Nothing. Forget it."

"No, what?" Moth insists.

Orazio looks at Moth again. They are similar in a way, only Moth is several years older. Maybe Orazio would be like him in seven years. Calm like him. Maybe not. "You ever get tired of sex?"

Not a question that Moth was expecting. He considers carefully the source. "It's the junk," he says.

"You think so?" Orazio asks hopefully.

Moth shrugs. "You know what it does."

"Hmm," Orazio says. He reaches up to pull the elastic from his hair, releasing the waves of glossy brown locks down around his shoulders. Hair down, he looks different, younger, almost child-like, his smooth-shaven face half-obscured, revealing only a slice of his face, the narrow chin and upturned nose. "Maybe I could cut back," he says, almost sincere.

"When did you start?" Moth asks.

"About… four years ago," Orazio says, surprising himself. "Yeah, four years."

"Like me," Moth says.

"Really? What made you start?"

Moth tells him about his ex shooting him up for the first time in the park.

"It was like that for me, too. A friend of mine. We'd gone to Rome with this other guy. We'd stayed up all night, went to a couple of places, discos. The next day we were driving home. They'd picked up before we left. I remember I was sitting in the backseat and my friend was in the front. He turned around to ask me if I wanted to try it. I didn't even think about it. I was too tired to think. I just said yes. I was seventeen."

Moth considers this. "What happened to your friend?"

"He moved to Rome. His brother lives there. The last I heard of him, he'd been in the hospital," Orazio says, putting out his cigarette. "Hep C."

"It happens," Moth says, for lack of anything else to say.

"But I'm fine," Orazio says, an afterthought.

"Are you?"

"I went for the test two months ago," Orazio explains. "Have you ever been tested?"

"I went last November," Moth says. "Came back negative."

"Can't be too careful," Orazio says. "Lots of nasty shit going around."

Moth wonders how careful Orazio is when he sells his body to lecherous old men, but he doesn't ask. When Orazio hit puberty, AIDS was already an established fact. Moth remembers the big scare, the beginning when it was still called "the gay disease." The paranoia. He was fourteen, on the verge of sexual activity. Moth was already fully aware of his attraction to other men by that point. Then along came this fucking disease which seemed to kill off only homosexual men. It had been devastating. Then the prejudice intensified. Throughout high school Moth had kept his sexuality a heavily-guarded secret. Living in a small town in the Midwest, there had been no other choice.

Orazio unlaces his boots and kicks them off. "What are you doing here?" he repeats.

"Your brother said I could crash here, if it's all right with you."

Orazio knows that Moth has nowhere else to go. "Yeah, sure," he says. He then gets up to turn on the stereo. In the deck is Moth's Garbage tape. Orazio pulls off his jeans and socks, singing along. "Come down to my house, stick a stone in your mouth. You can always pull out if you like it too much–" Orazio stops singing and tilts his head in Moth's direction. In English, he asks, "What does it mean: 'pull out'?"

"Ah… never mind," Moth says, smiling.

Orazio, in his t-shirt and boxers, gets into the bed. He tells Moth to pass him the cigarette. Then: "So it went all right tonight?"

Moth talks about the break-in. He hadn't had to pick the lock on the front door, having found it open. He'd gone in quietly since all was dark. He mentions running into Arturo, and going back to Arturo's house, then meeting Chiara.

"Chiara?" Orazio asks. "What's her last name?"

"I don't know, she didn't say."

"Short, dark hair, average height, glasses, kind of young?"

"Yeah."

"I know her," Orazio says. "She teaches in my faculty: political science. I've seen him, too."

"That figures," Moth murmurs.

"What?"

"Small towns are all alike," Moth says. "Everybody knows everybody."

"I know this Arturo by sight," Orazio says. "I don't know him." He considers and makes a face. "I don't want to know him."

"Why not?" Moth asks, feigning indifference.

"I don't like his face," Orazio says. "He's got the face of an asshole."

"Well," Moth says. A part of him would like to defend Arturo, but another part would rather keep quiet about his feelings instead of risking a jibing from Orazio's sharp little tongue. He recalls the earlier conversation with Juan, and it causes him to laugh.

"What?" Orazio asks.

"Nothing. I was just thinking about something Juan said."

"You saw Juan?"

"Yeah, tonight with your brother."

"Yeah, okay," Orazio says pensively.

"What's the matter? You don't trust him?"

Orazio quotes an old Italian adage: "Trusting is good, not trusting is better."

"Hmm," Moth says. "Orazio, you're a devil of a fellow."

"I know," he says.

SIX

Moth wakes up earlier than expected. Orazio had set the alarm clock because he, like his brother, had class in the morning. However, once awake, Moth, unlike Orazio, can't get back to sleep. He leaves Orazio still sleeping in the bed after he dresses and prepares a shot, then a cup of tea. Sam has already gone out. The apartment is silent apart from the sounds of traffic from the street below. Moth stands in the dirty kitchen, drinking the tea, smoking several cigarettes and trying not to think. Thinking is the last thing he wants to do. He tries to convince himself that today will be a better day than yesterday. It surely can't be any worse. Unconvinced, Moth quietly slips out of the apartment and goes to meet his social worker.

The social worker sees that Moth is high. She gives him a look that expresses disappointment but not surprise. She, of course, wants to talk about it. Moth, of course, does not. The subject of treatment is once again trotted out like a prized pony.

Moth says that he'll think about it, even though he won't. He wants to keep the social worker on his side because he might need her later for legal reasons. He answers her questions about his family somewhat vaguely. She then asks if he's involved with anyone.

"Qualcuna" – "anyone" in the feminine form.

He's told her about his junky ex, hasn't he? Or hasn't he? It is possible that he's talked about the first time he shot up without any reference to gender. He'd had a lot of conversations like that; it was word play. Saying "partner" instead of "boyfriend." Or "significant other." Or a more general "someone" instead of a "man." "I'm seeing someone..." Or maybe he had told her, and she'd forgotten. Anyway, his sexuality is none of her business. He says, simply, no.

Still, he is aware of how the past repeats itself, an endless loop, a Moebius strip. He was born in Urbino, he came back to Urbino. A loop, not a circle. If time were a circle, he would die in Urbino, close the circle, the cycle of birth, life and death. But, no, his intentions have always been to leave again. Maybe even to leave and come back again. It isn't the first time. He returned to London. He returned to California. He returned to Paris. He even returned to that little town in the Midwest, once, out of curiosity. And now he's returned to Urbino. This leaves only Boston to return to, the place he was most desperate to leave behind. Six years of bitter winters in New England had been enough.

But this infinite loop has more to do with just the place itself. Moth oscillates between big cities and little towns. Back in a little town, he misses the lures of the big city. Back in a little town, he feels fourteen or sixteen years old again, keeping his sexuality a secret. Or somewhat of a secret. Times have changed. Moth wonders, however, if he has changed. He senses his own ambiguity and blames it on the place.

He surprises himself with his own thoughts. What the hell is he thinking? It's not a secret. He doesn't feel shame, as Arturo would believe; he is motivated by survival, not shame. Homophobes were everywhere, but they are particularly proliferate in small towns like this one. Look at what those bastards did to that kid in Texas! Those guys in the park could have beaten him to death. He hadn't been able to fight back. What had the Stranger done to him?

Suddenly he realizes that he isn't listening to the social worker, hasn't heard a word she's said for a while now, lost in thoughts he didn't even want to have. He realizes he hasn't been listening because she's stopped talking, waiting for an answer to some unheard question. He excuses himself. He shouldn't have come here high, really, but he hadn't wanted to come junk sick. He'd half-expected that she would cancel the appointment once she'd seen his current condition. He'd seen a therapist back in Boston as part of a treatment program – at Quentin's insistence – where policy demanded that the client appear sober or be kicked out. Tough love without the love. His only formal attempt at kicking the habit for good.

She shuffles her papers. Moth, restless, looks at his wrist. Damn Orazio. Taking the watch and then last night. He had been lying in the bed in the dark next to Orazio – why had he slept in his jeans? Oh, yeah, no underwear – and Orazio said, in a very small voice, like a child: "Tell me I'm your best friend," so Moth replied: "Yes, you are my best friend," and then all was silent and both of them fell into an Orpheus sleep. It was like being in elementary school: *I'll be your best friend if you...*

Damn him.

The watch.

Quentin.

Quentin --- I swear I won't touch that shit again --- I promise you --- I'll get clean --- never again --- you can leave me if I'm lying --- have I ever lied to you? --- I mean it --- I'm through ---   God, don't cry --- I'm sorry, Quentin, I'm sorry, sorry, sorry ---

Appointment over. She's not available until next Tuesday at this time. Moth accepts the next appointment. She writes it down on her business card and hands it to him, as though she doesn't trust him to remember it on his own.

Outside, a light breeze. Moth walks over to the square. He half-expects to see Sam, but there is no one he knows. He sits down on the steps and smokes a cigarette. He has nowhere to go, nothing to do. This almost depresses him. He doesn't even have a book to read. What little he did have is at his brother's house.

He wonders how he can get his stuff back. He doesn't want to see Luciano. The desire to not see Luciano is stronger than the desire to have a clean pair of underwear. He decides to forget about the stuff. He has his little book of poems and a decent pair of shoes: black ankle boots with a side buckle by Ken Cole, comfortable and stylish. He knows from experience that a good pair of shoes is useful when one is homeless. Lots of walking involved in the pursuit of food, drugs, shelter, and cash—though he feels like he's getting too old to be on the streets. He has less energy than he used to. At least he has shelter and drugs. As for food, he hasn't eaten in a while, but, with the junk in him, he hasn't much appetite. Which leaves cash. He has few legal alternatives for obtaining cash. He's hesitant about the illegal alternatives. He'll have to think seriously about this. It's been years since he scammed anyone, and he's already in trouble with the law, in no position to take unnecessary risks.

While he is thinking about his options, he sees Arturo's girlfriend walk into the square. She's wearing a light-colored pantsuit and carrying a fat briefcase. When she sees him, he waves at her. *Why not?* She comes over to him, and he rises to take the hand she offers. She asks him how he's doing.

"Not bad," he says.

"I'm on break," she tells him. "I was just on my way to the bar for something to drink. Would you care to join me, or are you expecting someone?"

"Well, I…" Moth says. He hesitates, wondering why she's being so friendly. "No, I'm not expecting anyone."

They step over to the bar. Moth opens the door for her. They stand at the counter. He checks his change and orders a *caffe macchiato* from the bartender who looks very familiar. In this different light, it takes Moth a few seconds to place his face: Juan's friend from the club. *The asshole.*

Chiara asks for a pineapple juice.

"You don't drink coffee?" Moth asks, feeling out of place. Not because he is having a drink with a woman, but because she is Arturo's woman. He wonders what they talked about last night after he left.

"Coffee? No. It makes me jittery," she says, setting her bag down by her feet. "Arturo doesn't either. He doesn't like it."

That makes two things that Arturo doesn't like, Moth muses.

"So, it is difficult for you, being back in Urbino?" she asks.

Small talk. Moth can make small talk. He used to be quite good at it, in another life. "It's strange."

"It's not very exciting here, is it?"

"Not very."

The bartender brings the drinks and brief eye contact. Moth can't remember his name, although it was an unusual name for an Italian boy. At least he knows now how he recognized him at the club. "*Grazie*," Moth says.

The smallest hint of a smile. "*Prego*," says the bartender and returns to work. Moth tilts two spoons worth of sugar into the cup. He misses

American coffee. There was something comforting about the large hot paper cup in the hand on a winter morning on the way to work.

"Where were you living before?" Chiara asks.

"In America," he says. "Boston."

"How long were you in Boston?"

"About six years."

"Did you go to school there?"

"No, I went to school in California," Moth says, then adds, "Berkeley."

"Graduated?"

"English literature."

"School in America is expensive, isn't it?"

"I had a scholarship," Moth says.

Through her glasses, her dark eyes, lively and warm, rest on Moth's face. *What does she see?* he wonders, not caring much. Maybe she's impressed that he graduated from Berkeley. Except that he hadn't. He'd gradually lost interest in his studies. His grades had started slipping in his third year, after he'd returned from London the second time, where he'd spent six months studying theater – mostly Shakespeare. After the continuous party which was his London experience, and the exhilarating freedom from his family, he'd found it difficult to return to campus and bury himself in the books again, to exist back under the influence of his father. His father hadn't approved of Moth's choice of study. A folly. Unlike Luciano, who had already finished his doctorate and had started practicing law.

"You were working in Boston?" Chiara asks.

"For a publishing company."

"Editing?"

He hadn't realized he was playing Twenty Questions. He wondered what conclusion she would reach at the end. "No. Typesetting, design. Computer work."

"You're good with computers?"

"Yeah."

"Do you know how to use the Internet?"

"Sure."

"Maybe you could help Arturo," she says. "He's down at the library right now. He wanted to do some research on the Internet, but he doesn't know much about computers. If you're free, I mean. I'm sure he would appreciate some help."

This was getting odder by the moment. "Right now?" he asks and she responds in the affirmative. "Shouldn't he be at work?"

"He took the day off," she says. She checks her watch, then says that she has to go. At the cash register, Moth reaches into his pocket, but she waves his money away, saying that she'll cover the coffee. As she rummages around in her bag, Moth scans the bar. He watches Juan's friend for a moment – crisp black pants, apron clean and stiff, a stylish white shirt which drapes perfectly, perfect posture, tray balanced in one hand – as he whips his rag through the air and leans over to wipe down a table for a pair of admiring American girls.

Outside on the steps, Chiara smiles and tells Moth to give Romeo her love, like that, as if she were certain that he would go.

Watching her slip through the crowd, he lights up a cigarette. *Romeo.* He'd played Romeo in London one night when they'd all been drinking in the courtyard of the apartment building where they lived, all the American students. They'd studied the life out of that play. He can't remember if they had been drinking for a particular reason or just to get drunk. His friend – *what was her name?* – Sara, maybe, had been standing on the balcony of her apartment on the second floor, with a beer and a cigarette, looking down in the courtyard. And what had he been doing? Maybe drinking the Baileys she had given him out of a plastic thermos, shooting the shit with some of the guys, laughing. Moth had drunk a lot of Baileys with this girl. She was totally cool, intelligent, witty, and always willing to hit the pubs when no one else was. She proclaimed herself an atheist. Moth considered himself agnostic at that point. On the fence, so to speak, unwilling to return to his Catholic roots yet hesitant to renounce all of it, give up God completely. They'd had one hell of a conversation about God in that little pub out by the Heath.

In the courtyard, one of the guys called out, *Hey, it's Juliet up there on her balcony,* and everyone had laughed. The girl had heard them. She leaned out over the railing and started:

Romeo, Romeo, wherefore art thou, Romeo? The whole passage, by heart. Moth, of course, also knew the passage by heart. He stepped forward: *What light through yonder window breaks?* and so on. The others grew completely silent as they recited the whole scene, up to the kissing part. Then the others started shouting at him: *Go, Romeo!* so Moth climbed up the side of the apartment building to the balcony to reach her. He kissed her cheek. The crowd roared. Moth climbed down and everyone cracked up completely. After that, whenever the guys saw him, it was always: *Go Romeo!*

She was the only person who had perceived Moth's crush on one of the other boys in their program, Paul. Moth had spent a lot of time with Paul, without ever confessing the extent of his feelings. It had been a grand lesson in frustration.

Frustration. Of course he'll go see Arturo. Frustration makes good poetry.

What had happened to the girl? Or to Paul? He'd seen Paul once or twice on campus after that. Then, he had no idea. People kept disappearing out of his life, extinguished like flames, leaving only a smoky trace.

He strolls down the street to the library. Inside, he sees Arturo sitting at one of the computers in the foyer. He's wearing brown jeans and a different gray turtleneck sweater, darker than the last, a brown leather jacket draped over the empty chair beside him. Moth walks over and sits down in the chair after moving the jacket aside. Arturo looks at him questioningly. Moth tells him that Juliet sends her love.

"Who?"

"Your girlfriend sent me down here."

"When did you talk to my girlfriend?" Arturo asks.

"Just now, in the square," Moth says. Seeing Arturo's expression, he adds, "You don't have to be jealous."

Arturo regards Moth for a moment, rubbing his jaw thoughtfully. "That's very amusing," he says, in a way that doesn't seem complimentary.

Moth doesn't know what to say. He feels annoyed with Arturo, like he knows that Arturo has put up some psychological barrier between them that alters his appearance, that he's hiding himself behind a mask, a tough front, like Juan, and underneath he's just as creamy and sweet and soft as a chocolate silk pie. *Maybe we're all like that,* Moth thinks: *masked.* The idea curdles his thoughts. He is full of the desire to smash Arturo's mask, and stare at the real face beneath.

However, smashing someone's mask requires a lot more than just a blunt instrument. It requires good aim and good timing. His timing is no good. His best bet is to be civil, kill some time, compose a poem in his head.

Moth gestures at the screen. "What are you looking for here?"

"You know what I'm looking for," Arturo says, "but I just can't find anything."

"Did you try the newspapers?"

"The newspapers?"

"I bet that some of them have their archives on the Internet. You can go in and search."

Arturo regards Moth for a moment, thinking that he might be useful. "How do I do that?"

"We can start with a search engine."

"A what?"

"Click up here," Moth says, pointing. He tells Arturo what to type in. Moth maneuvers him through the archives of a larger Italian newspaper. At the search engine within the newspaper, Arturo types in the word "gold." A few moments pass, the flicker of the terminal, then the screen is flooded with thousands of documents ranging from the stock market to the British crown jewels.

"Fuck," Arturo murmurs. "Now what?"

"Go back," Moth says.

They try again, adding "eyes" to the search. Again they wait while the engine sorts through innumerable documents. Hundreds of articles appear listed on the screen. Arturo thinks for a moment, then, unassisted, returns to the preceding page to add another word to the equation Gold + eyes + death.

Six documents come up. Arturo and Moth scan through them. Half of them deal with an accident in an African gold mine. The other half deal with an unsolved murder of a young man in Riccione. Arturo clicks on the first file and they read. Then the second, then the third. He reopens the first file, which was the longest and most detailed of the three. He skims it once more, then looks at Moth.

"Well?" Arturo says.

Moth's eyes linger on the description of the suspect, seen leaving the scene of the crime. One meter ninety: tall, slight build: slim; fair complexion: pale. Long black hair and gold-colored eyes. It could be Moth's Stranger.

It could be anybody.

Moth meets Arturo's gaze. "I don't know."

Arturo taps his fingers against the table. "Can I print this?"

Moth glances around, searching for a printer and, not seeing one, says, "I don't know."

Arturo swivels in the chair. "Hang on a second."

Moth watches Arturo get up and cross the room to the librarian's desk. He speaks briefly to the girl behind it, then walks back to the computers. He moves the cursor to the print icon and clicks on it. Beyond the desk, the electric whir of the printer. Arturo picks up his jacket and puts it on. Moth stands up and follows him to the desk.

Arturo pays for the copies, folds them, and places them in his pocket.

"Now what are you going to do?" Moth asks.

Arturo withdraws a cellular phone from his pocket, flips it open, checking for messages. "Now I'm going home."

"I mean, what are you going to do with this information?"

Arturo thinks for a moment. He'd rather not talk here. He closes the phone and puts it back in his pocket, and gestures toward the stairs. "Come on."

Outside on the street, they stop. Moth can see how Arturo is stalling, debating on something. Moth waits for something harsh to come out of Arturo's mouth. The last thing he expects is any semblance of gratitude for the help he's given. He's noticed how much easier it is to be cruel than to be kind. Or maybe it's just better to be pessimistic: less disappointment that way.

Arturo realizes that Moth is involved as much as anyone could be, and that makes him useful. "I think it's a good idea to talk to the witness."

"The article didn't name the witness."

"I know it didn't name the witness. But who is the most likely to see someone who is leaving an apartment in the middle of the night?"

"A neighbor."

"Exactly," Arturo says. "Are you free tomorrow?"

Moth is always free, but he doesn't say this. "Yeah. Why?"

"Come with me to Riccione. We'll do some private investigating."

"You have a car?"

"Yeah."

Moth pretends to think about it. "What time?"

"We'll leave around noon."

"Yeah, I guess so."

"I'll pick you up at Porta Lavagine, then," Arturo says. "You know which one that is?"

Moth points in the general direction of Porta Lavagine. "The one down at the bottom of the hill there, with the record store near it."

"Right," Arturo says. He checks his watch. "I've got to go. See you tomorrow."

Moth watches Arturo leave, a poem half-formed in his heart.

~

Night. In front of The Dive. He wonders what he's doing on the threshold, neither inside nor out. On the border. No one's around so he speaks aloud, "What am I doing here?" as if speaking the words aloud would clarify the situation. They don't clarify shit. He still doesn't know. The Stranger flits through his mind, tugging at him the way water draws the rod, or the moon, the tide. Moth is liquid, swirling, churning all around himself. He briefly touches his right wrist, tracing the tail of his dragon, as if checking to see if it's still under his skin or has somehow vanished, like a watch in a drug deal. He is liquid on a slope, being pulled down, water in a basin, being sucked through a drain. He feels drawn to The Dive, but he resists.

Someone once said that resistance is futile. He can't remember who said that. He is about to step through the door of the club when Orazio, followed by Juan, steps out.

Orazio has the reckless air about him of someone who is very high on junk, and seems too pleased to see Moth, a sparkling slash of a smile blooming out of his lips. "Hey, what are you doing?"

"I was just about to go in," Moth admits.

Orazio and Juan exchange a glance, thick as thieves, smug. "You don't want to go in there," Orazio says.

"No, you don't want to go in there," Juan echoes.

Moth has the sense of being outside of something. "Is there anyone in there?" he asks, vague.

"Nah, no one," Orazio says. "Not even a dog." He fumbles in his jacket for a cigarette. "Well, the only dog was Juan."

"Yeah, I was the only dog," Juan agrees.

In English, Orazio says, "The big dog."

"What?" Juan asks.

Moth translates.

"Oh, right," Juan says. "Woof."

"Anyway, no one's down there," Orazio repeats.

"Thursday night," Juan says. "Everyone's down at the Portico."

"Is that where you're going?" Moth asks.

"Yeah, Sam's supposed to be down there," Orazio says. "You coming?"

Moth considers. Unable to make his own decision, letting someone make the decision for him seemed like the reasonable thing to do. "Yeah, sure."

Orazio starts moving suddenly as if he'd been jump-started. "Okay. Let's go," he says decisively, more to the street in front of him than to the men behind him. Dog-like, Moth and Juan trail after him. Within moments, Orazio is several paces ahead of them, not looking back.

Juan gives Moth a sharp, sober look. "I'd keep an eye on your friend there, if I were you."

Moth's gaze flickers up towards Orazio, moving with less bounce and more purpose in his stride. "What do you mean?"

"Let's just say that certain people tend to exaggerate sometimes."

"Ah," Moth says. So he's been appointed the new baby-sitter. He considers Juan for a moment. "And are you ever victim to the tendency to exaggerate?"

Juan smiles. "Sam's right. He said that you're not so keen on making statements as you are on posing questions. Don't you ever just make a statement?"

"I make my statements in other ways."

"I understand what you mean," Juan says.

Orazio glances over his shoulder and calls back, "Come on!"

"Yes, sir!" Juan says.

They arrive at the Portico. The bar is already crowded. All arcs and pale stone, Moth thinks that it must have been a wine cellar before it was transformed into a bar. They weave among the bodies and the techno throb to find Sam and Lisa sharing a cloudy-looking cocktail, sickly green like flu phlegm, in one of the alcoves. Greetings and some conversation. Moth doesn't feel like talking so he lights a cigarette and watches the people on the dance floor. He realizes that he'd rather not be here, but, at the same time, he has nowhere else to go. At some point, Orazio places a glass of wine in his hand, so he drinks it. Then Orazio disappears. Ten minutes later, Orazio comes back.

"I've got to go," Orazio shouts at the group over the music.

Before he can run off, Moth stops him, leaning closer to the younger man's ear. "Where are you going?"

"The Dive. I'll be back in ten minutes."

"I'll go with you." Orazio gives him a suspicious look, causing him to add, "I don't want to stay here."

Orazio waves to the others and leaves with Moth. Outside, he realizes how steamy and claustrophobic the Portico was, when the cool air and black sky strike him.

"I'll only be at The Dive for a minute," Orazio reveals.

"Yeah, fine," Moth says, now keeping up with his friend's quick pace. "What were you and Juan doing?"

"Nothing," Orazio says. "I just ran into him at The Dive. For like five minutes, then we left."

"That's strange."

Orazio turns his head. "What's strange?"

"Juan told me that I should keep an eye on you."

Orazio makes a face like a bug just flew into his mouth. "Fuck him," he murmurs. "He does that. Tries to be everybody's mother. How many mothers does a guy need?"

"One," Moth says, "although Juan might look good in a house dress."

Orazio considers this and laughs. "How about a tight leather skirt?"

"Blood red lipstick."

"Stiletto heels."

"And a pink lace bra."

They burst out laughing.

"Fish net stockings," Orazio adds and they laugh again.

The arrive at The Dive. "What do you need to do here?" Moth asks.

"See a guy," Orazio says, in a way that Moth understands that it is drug, and not sex, related. "You coming in or will you wait here?"

Like sex, drug deals are also a private act. "I'll wait inside, at the bar," Moth says.

"All right."

Orazio leaves Moth at the bar and gestures to a guy waiting at a table, "junky" written all over him. Moth watches as they exchange a few words, then the junky gets up from the table and follows Orazio out the back. He could time the transaction. Two minutes. He looks at his naked wrist, from habit still.

A voice hums in his ear. "It's ten past one."

Moth doesn't dare turn. Instead, he raises his eyes to the mirror behind the bar and sees the Stranger beside him. The Stranger meets his gaze in the mirror and smiles a diabolic smile, which causes the sluggish blood in Moth's veins to race. Moth doesn't turn, unable to break the contact established in the looking glass. "What are you doing here?"

The Stranger leans closer. Moth feels the thick black hair of the Stranger brush against his face, as he sees it reflected. "I was looking for you."

"I mean…" Moth starts and then hesitates. His throat is blocked. He swallows slowly. "The cops are looking for you."

"So I've read," the Stranger says. "Did you think I wouldn't read the papers? Is that what you thought? Is that why you talked?"

Along with Moth's desire, a dread is growing. "I didn't talk," he manages.

"You're a liar," the Stranger says. His voice is calm, deep, smooth. "Do you know what they do to liars in some places? They rip out the offending tongue." Moth watches as the Stranger's pale hand flashes through the dark, to Moth's mouth, the fingers infiltrating, filling Moth's mouth with a bitter taste of which he is aware for only a brief moment before he is overwhelmed by the throb of pleasure which rages through his body as before, growing fast and furious, his stomach hot, limbs heavy, cock straining against his jeans, on the brink of an orgasm. The Stranger suddenly removes his hand from within Moth's mouth.

Moth's senses return to him slowly. "I didn't talk," he repeats.

The Stranger takes hold of Moth's jacket, jerking Moth to face him. He stares into Moth's eyes for a moment, then releases him. "Good," he says.

Moth's breath rushes out of him.

"Come on," the Stranger says. "There's something I want to do to you."

The warning bell that has been steadily ringing in Moth's head since the beginning of this encounter intensifies. Moth ignores it. "Oh, yeah? What?"

The Stranger smiles again, filling Moth with a longing, unbearable in its intensity. "I'm going to fuck you to death."

Moth's mind shuts down. And then the blur. His body follows the Stranger out into Rats' Alley, into a particularly dark alcove, limp as water under the touch of the Stranger. He shivers and throbs, tension stiffening his body as the Stranger runs his tongue up his neck. His balls aching, Moth clings to the pale white neck, pulling the Stranger closer.

With the Stranger's mouth against his own, Moth explodes in an orgasm as violent as the last, his groans caught in the Stranger's mouth. Weak-kneed, he clings to the slim body of the Stranger, a bitter taste in his mouth like the taste of heroin – heroin, yes, that's what it's like – but he cannot think about this, he cannot think about anything, lost in the demand of his body to have more. Hands skim his naked skin as the Stranger pushes up his shirt, then tongue to aching nipple, the left one, the tug of the Stranger's teeth on his nipple ring sends him into another spasm, waves of painful pleasure, which still do not satisfy the desperate need. His head spins, thick as muck, unbearable and terrible and wonderful. He is liquid in the arms of the Stranger, sloshing everywhere in a raging torrent of desire.

Hot breath against his ear, the Stranger asks, "Do you want me?"

Moth's thoughts are honey, sticky and thick. He wants. There exists nothing but this need "Want–" he gasps.

"I'm going to fuck you to death."

"Fuck me to death."

The loosening of his belt. Already, Moth has disappeared. Moth has ceased to exist. Aware of the increasing need, the demand, the penetration, being taken against the wall, his empty orgasms improbably bursting out, rolling out one after the other, his body burns, melts, is all, is nothing. He doesn't feel the cold stone against his hands, nor the cold air against his skin; he drowns within the sensation. His heart weakens. He stops breathing.

Then a sharp stab within his bowels, a hot, fast, metallic pain like a knife puncture in his gut. But he has no breath with which to cry out, no strength to force the air out of his lungs. He is choking with the pain, but only for a moment before a flood of sweet darkness enfolds him, and whatever was left of him slips away into the vast black nothing.

~

While Moth is being fucked to death by a Stranger in Rats' Alley, there is absolutely no one in the world who is thinking about him. Juan is watching a young, blond girl, probably foreign, American, or maybe

German, who is sitting with another girl, brunette, in the Portico. He is thinking about how he'd like to meet her, and what he would like to do after he meets her.

Sam is looking at Lisa, wondering if she's drunk, and feeling slightly tipsy himself. Lisa is not one of the three women he's slept with, but he would like her to become the fourth. He thinks that she's kind of strange, and he likes that. But he's too shy to make the first move.

Lisa is thinking about how bored she is, and how she'd like to have something to relieve the boredom. She's pretty sure that Sam could get something from his brother, but she won't ask yet. Maybe after he makes a move.

Arturo is at home, while Chiara sleeps beside him in the bed, thinking about how lovely she looks when she sleeps – sweet, young, angelic – and half-wondering why he doesn't propose to her, make their engagement official with a ring. He has enough money stashed in the bank to be able to buy her something appropriate, if not extravagant.

Orazio, wherever he may be, is thinking about how he would like another fix, even though the last one hasn't worn off yet.

And, as for what the Stranger thinks, only the Stranger knows.

~

Moth comes to slowly. At first he's only aware of the cold that has seeped in through his clothes, down to his bones. He finds himself lying in one of the alcoves of Rats' Alley, face down on the ground, amid the refuse of empty beer bottles, cigarette butts, discarded syringes and used condoms. It's enough to make a man vomit, which is what he promptly does.

After the heaving subsides, he manages to pull himself to his feet. He places a hand against the wall to steady himself. He can't feel his legs. For that matter, he can't feel anything other than the cold. He tries to figure out what happened, but his head is hazy. He can't remember how he got here.

He looks around and at himself. His shirt has been torn, but he can't recall how. He tries to remember who he is. It takes a moment, but his own name eventually comes back to him, like an obedient dog being called over by its owner. He releases the wall, and then falls back down to his knees. He doesn't feel the impact.

He pulls himself back up slowly. He wonders why he can't feel his body. He wracks his useless brain. The last thing that he remembers was coming to The Dive with Orazio.

Orazio, yes, he thinks. *I must have had an overdose. That explains it.*

He doesn't remember shooting up, but why else would he be in Rats' Alley? It wouldn't be the first time he'd had an overdose. The last time he'd been with some people he didn't know, and his ex. They'd picked him up off the floor. His ex had slapped him hard across the face to snap him out of it. That experience had always remained fuzzy in his memory. They had made him walk around to get the blood moving, and it had been enough.

Moth decides to get moving. He has no idea how long he'd been lying unconscious on the ground. Using the wall as his support, he inches his way out of the alley, heading towards Orazio's house.

After an eternity of stumbling and vomiting his way up Via Rafaello, he rings the front door. Sam buzzes him in, watching as Moth drags himself up the stairs.

"Orazio?" Moth manages to mumble.

"I thought he was with you," Sam says. He steps back to let Moth enter, staring at him. "Man, you are fucked-up," Sam says.

Moth grunts in reply, drags himself over to Orazio's bed, and passes out.

~

He dreams a river of words. Rapids of verbs. Whirlpools of modals. Determiners bubbling through silver filaments of noncountable nouns. Waves of modifiers. And he is dressed all in black at the mossy bank of the river, watching the words as they flow by him. He bends down for a closer look. There are undulations in the currents of countable nouns all mixed in with the adjectives. He reaches in and plucks out a word. It is slippery in his hand, hard to hold onto without a net. He considers the word. LANDSCAPE. He places it on the bank beside him. It flops, gasping like a fish. The words are alive. Living language. Instinctively he knows that beyond the bend of the river there are stagnant pools with dead words, dead language, a mire of Latin, Sanskrit, ancient Greek. He fishes out another word. GREEN. He doesn't like the look of this word. It glares, vibrant, moving in a snaky manner with hidden connotations. He throws GREEN back into the river. He fishes again and again. He is a fisher of words, not men. He keeps THE. A most useful article. Fishing, he pulls out two words stuck together, white and smooth and shimmering. YOUR BODY. He places YOUR BODY on the bank and regards what he has selected: LANDSCAPE THE YOUR BODY.

Your body the landscape.

He wakes. The only light in the room is from the other room. He looks at the alarm clock. It's just past three o'clock. He doesn't know whether it's night or day, whether a lot of time has passed or only a little, but that doesn't have importance to him now. The only thing that matters is the poem. It's all there in his head, fully formed. All he has to do is give birth to it. He switches on the lamp and takes his little book out and writes.

Your body the landscape. He is a man in a reverie. The river of words – black, jagged little words burning through the page – pours out automatically. His mind is completely focused on the task at hand. His face a grimace of total concentration. His penmanship is sharp and clear, decisive strokes embedded in the paper. Line after line, without pause, leaps out of the nib of the Pentel in his hand, which turns pale from the force and determination of his grip. He writes, he writes, and then –

The front door slams shut. Moth comes out of his reverie. He stares, fixated on the page. He can't remember what he was about to write. He has no idea where he'd been going. Lost, all lost. So Kubla Khan, it was ridiculous.

Orazio's voice, from the other room. "Hey."

Sam: "Hey."

"*Farfalla?*"

"I thought he was with you."

"Obviously he isn't."

"Just kidding. He's in the bedroom."

"Yeah?" Pause. "How is he?"

"He's all fucked up."

"What do you mean, all fucked up?"

"I mean totally fucked up."

"Totally?" A long pause. "What are you doing?"

"I'm staring at the wall."

An extremely long pause.

"Why?"

"Because I like it."

A shorter pause. "Jesus Christ."

Orazio leans into the bedroom, sees Moth sitting fully dressed on the bed. He comes in, closing the door behind him. "Don't tell me you're staring at the wall, too."

"As a matter of fact, no," Moth says. "Got a cigarette?"

Orazio comes over and sits next to Moth, handing him a Marlboro. "Jesus Christ," he mutters again. "That brother of mine. I think he's on something."

Moth admires how Orazio can say such things with such sincerity. "It's possible."

Orazio's eyes flicker up and down over Moth in assess mode. "I mean on something strange," he says. "Something beyond the norm."

Orazio's phrase, so casually tossed off, strikes Moth. A vision flashes through his mind. The Stranger within him. Moth strangled by pleasure. A fuzzy recollection, better than nothing. Drugs and sex. Halfway beyond the norm. Or... something.

Seeing Moth's grave expression, Orazio says, "Hey, I'm sorry I took off like that. The guy I met didn't have all the money, so I went with him to his friend's house to get it. Halfway to Fano, I swear. What an asshole. You're not mad, are you?"

Orazio is looking at him with that same sincerity, him the type of boy who'd help somebody's grandmother across the street before stealing her purse. He should have gone into acting instead of hustling. Or maybe it was the same thing. "Nah. Forget it."

"What did you do?"

Moth feels secretive about what he'd done and with whom he'd done it. "Nothing, really. Hung around, came back here, wrote a poem."

Orazio thinks about this. He has no idea what Moth writes about. "Could you read it to me?"

Moth looks down at the book still open against his thigh. "Well, it's not finished."

"That doesn't matter."

"It's in English."

"I don't care."

He's run out of reasons to say no. *Why not?* "All right, then."

Orazio listens as Moth reads. Moth doesn't have a very deep voice, and he is usually soft-spoken, but, when he reads the poem, his voice becomes clear and powerful. Orazio doesn't understand all the words, but it hardly matters. The poem has an unrelenting slow rhythm which draws him in. He understands the subject: the body of a man, described as a landscape, both lush and arid, foreign territory ravished, then the response of the beautiful body as it is explored by eyes and hands and lips, a poem infused with sex, with longing and passion, satiating and satisfying but also cruel, a cruel body, cruel because of its beauty, but still warm and enticing, arousing, tempting, responding to the eyes and hands and lips, the body with its writhing torrents of oil black hair, and its eyes cool green Buddhas beckoning, demanding blind worship, promising –

The poem ends suddenly, hanging in the air. After a moment, Moth closes the book and sets it aside. "That's it." He watches Orazio thinking. "Did you like it?"

"Yeah, I did," Orazio says. He stares at Moth for a moment, not speaking. Maybe about to speak. Maybe thinking about speaking, but not actually doing so.

"What?" Moth prompts.

Orazio turns away. He starts to unlace his boots, kicks them off, then sighs. "Fuck, I'm tired."

"Then sleep."

"You, too?"

"Exhausted, to tell the truth."

"A guy wouldn't lie about a thing like that." Orazio stands up, taking off his coat. He walks over to the door, opens it, and sticks his head out. "Jesus Christ, Sam, go to bed."

"Yeah, good night, Orazio. Good night, *Farfalla*. Good night, everyone," Sam calls back.

Satisfied, Orazio shuts the door and pulls off his shirt, then his jeans. Meanwhile, Moth undresses – except for his dirty jeans – and lies back on the bed. He glances at Orazio, standing by the door, adjusting his boxer shorts. Moth is surprised to notice that within Orazio's boxers is a rather lively erection straining against the cotton. Orazio catches Moth's trailing eye and fixes him with a challenging look.

"What the hell is that?" Moth asks.

"Eh, I don't know," Orazio says, then climbs into the bed, turning his back to Moth, and reaching to turn out the light. "It's not in my control."

Then darkness. Moth thinks, *Maybe it was the poem,* and immediately falls asleep.

SEVEN

Moth awakens. Again there is only the light from the other room, but this time, Moth perceives the quality of light as not being artificial. The space beside him in the bed is cold. He sits up, blinking, and reaches for the alarm clock. It's 12:00. He thinks about time for a moment, how it can rush by, how it can freeze a moment into permanent memory, how it can be lost like a wallet. He recalls what Marguerite Duras once wrote, that the best way to use time was to waste it. Words which he was living by. Wasting time, with nothing to do, time lost its meaning. Let other people be slaves to the hours, hurrying from one appointment to the other.

A switch suddenly flicks in Moth's memory. *12:00. Appointment. Arturo!*

He scrambles out of the bed, cursing. He throws on his Ken Cole boots, grabs his shirt, considers the rip in it, then tosses it aside. He looks in Orazio's surprisingly spacious closet and steals a dark blue v-neck t-shirt with barely a thought, pulling it on as he moves back to the bedroom. He picks up his jacket and catches a glimpse of himself in the mirror, puffy eyes and disheveled hair, face unnaturally pale. He looks terrible. Spotting Sam's sunglasses on the floor, Moth decides to borrow them. He is already running down the stairs before the sunglasses are on his face.

Five minutes later, he arrives at Porta Lavagine. He scans the cars parked all around the wall. A blue Fiat flashes its headlights at him: Arturo, waiting for him at the curve. Moth walks over and gets in.

"Seat belt," Arturo says in lieu of a greeting, and pulls out into the street, while Moth fiddles with the seat belt, wondering about Arturo's driving skills. He contemplates the possibility of Arturo knocking more of his teeth out, this time against the dashboard in a grisly car accident, which then leads his mind to a fantastic Ballardesque image of their mangled bodies, meshed with metal wreckage, entwined on the dusty asphalt under the clear blue sky.

But this premonition is soon dispelled. Arturo drives carefully enough, his green eyes darting from the road to rearview to side mirror and back again. In silence, they pass the Chinese restaurant at the bend in the road; at the intersection they turn left towards Pesaro.

He looks at Arturo from the corner of his eye. Brown shirt of an expensive-looking material with a high collar, over dark, subtly-checked pants of a light wool, and a fine pair of shoes. Hair slicked back a bit, barely under control. Clean shaven. He looks good. Moth wants to ask him what the occasion is, but decides not to. A compliment is out of the question as well. Looking at Arturo, he thinks about the poem he was writing last night. He's already forgotten how it went. As he reaches into his pocket, he realizes that he's left his little book of poems by Orazio's bed. In the rush to meet Arturo, he'd not only forgotten the book, but he'd had no time to have his morning cup of tea, nor a cigarette, nor a shot.

His thoughts focus on this one fact, like a pinpoint of light at the end of a long, black tunnel. Odd that he'd forgotten. More than odd, extremely unusual. Moth does a mental check-up of his body. He doesn't feel junk sick. He feels slightly agitated, but that might be resolved by a few cigarettes. Or it might be his mind, which feels slightly foggy, half-there, leaping from the surface of one subject to the surface of another, but never descending far enough below as to be profound. Like this morning he'd awoken thinking about time. Surface thinking, nothing profound. Wasting time and losing time. He had lost some time. Why didn't that concern him?

A blue T sign catches Moth's attention. The tobacco shop. This increases his desire for a cigarette. He checks his pockets. No cigarettes. Had he seen Arturo smoking? "You don't have a cigarette, do you?"

Arturo glances at him. "Check the glove compartment."

Moth opens the glove compartment. A wad of documents crushed by a rubber band, a yellow pencil without a point, and a pack of Marlboro lights, more than half full. Moth takes one, pressing the car lighter, waiting impatiently for it to pop back out. "Do you want one?"

"I don't really smoke," Arturo says. Then, as an afterthought, adds, "A friend of mine left his cigarettes in the car. Forgot them."

"Then I thank your friend," Moth says. The lighter pops back out and Moth yanks it from its hole, pressing the cherry-red glow of the hot metal to the tip of his cigarette. Lit, he cranks open the window a crack, and leans back, looking out. Greening hills full of sunflowers waiting to bloom and become a postcard. The occasional bar or gas station, or a combination of the two. But mostly what he sees are the trees, new leaves forming at the tips of the bare branches, scrawny cheerleaders waving green pom-poms. Trees and hills and cultivated fields.

Into the small town of Trasanni, then out again. Moth tosses his cigarette butt out the window, thinking about the fact that he's sitting in the car with Arturo, with his head in a fog and nothing to say. Maybe he should have had his morning cup of tea. Maybe the caffeine would have helped. Or better yet, a nice, strong espresso to get his sluggish blood to flow. Yes, now that he thinks about it, some coffee would be really good right now. He looks at Arturo, green eyes on the road and both hands on the wheel, still thinking about an espresso, the black liquid contrasting in a perfect circle in the tiny white cup on white saucer, a bit of light brown foam.

Arturo casts him a quick sidelong glance and asks, "Want to stop for a coffee?"

The sign for the next town looms up: Gallo. Surely Moth has been on this road before, on the bus from Pesaro when he arrived a few months earlier, but he doesn't remember it. It gives him a strange sensation to see his last name in bold letters on the white sign, even though it's probably just a coincidence. In English, Gallo meant rooster, which left Moth open to all sorts of cock jokes, so he usually left his name untranslated. And a rooster was such a useless beast, good for stud, unable to even fly. A most unromantic name to have, but at least it sounded good in Italian.

So they stop in rooster town at a small bar and order two straight *espressi*. Moth watches Arturo stirs in two large spoonfuls of sugar as

Moth watches, propping Sam's sunglasses up on his head in the Italian man fashion. "I thought you didn't drink coffee."

Arturo shrugs. "I don't usually," he says, setting the spoon down on the saucer. "One after lunch, every now and then." He narrows his eyes at Moth. "What made you ask me that, anyway?"

"That's what your girlfriend said."

Arturo smiles slightly. "And what else did my girlfriend say?"

"Nothing, really. She asked me a lot of questions."

"Ah," Arturo says. "That doesn't surprise me."

They both sip their coffee. Sweet and bitter on Moth's tongue, reminding him that he hadn't brushed his teeth. Personal hygiene hasn't been in his top ten priorities lately, and he can't remember the last time he even showered. Better not to think about it. At least the dark stubble on his jaw conforms with Italian male fashion.

Arturo sets down his cup. "Ready?"

"Almost," Moth replies and finishes the coffee, pays for his with the last of his money, and follows Arturo out to the car. Once they are back on the road, Moth rolls down the window and lights another cigarette, his head a little less in the fog. He looks at Arturo. "Did you go to work today?"

"For an hour," Arturo replies.

Moth considers asking about his brother but feels too apprehensive about Arturo's possible responses to actually bring himself to do so.

Arturo wonders if Moth cares about what Luciano is going through, but Arturo knows better than to entangle himself in a family feud and doesn't plan on offering any information to either brother, even if asked. Fortunately, Moth doesn't ask. Arturo abruptly changes the subject. "Do you mind if I put on some music?"

"It's your car."

Arturo pops in a dance compilation tape. Throbbing beat and synthesizer pour out of the speakers, rattling both their spines a little.

"You like this kind of music?" Moth asks.

Arturo counters with, "Why? You don't?"

Not wanting to criticize, Moth says, "I prefer my music more… alternative."

"There aren't too many discos with that kind of music."

"I don't spend too much time in discos."

"Oh, really?"

"I used to go dancing all the time when I was younger," Moth offers, slightly relieved. Music was usually a safe subject. "In America, there were places with good music. The kind I like, I mean."

"Well, I know there's a place up in Rimini that has that kind of music," Arturo says. "I can't remember the name of the place. I've only been there once, and that was a long time ago."

"Well, I don't get out of Urbino much, so I guess it doesn't matter."

"There aren't too many good places to dance in Urbino," Arturo says.

"Yeah, I've noticed that."

Arturo knows that Chiara told him where Moth came from, but he hadn't been paying much attention to the details. "Where in America were you living?"

"I was in Boston before I came here."

Arturo wracks his brain but North American geography isn't one of his strong points. "Boston – what's it near?"

"It's a few hours north of New York," Moth says. The three pieces of America, he's learned, familiar to all Italians are New York, California and – for some unknown reason – Texas. Everything else in-between was a blur, an empty mass of land.

"Ah," Arturo says. "It's a big city, isn't it?"

"There's about three million people."

"Three million," Arturo repeats. It's a staggering number of people. "You know, there's about twelve thousand people in Urbino."

And nothing around for miles, Moth thinks.

"It must have been interesting there," Arturo says.

"There were some good places to hang out."

Arturo contemplates an American city that large. He has only the American movies to feed his imagination. He pictures gray, a cluster of tall buildings, very wide roads full of large American cars, neon everywhere, and the distinctly American scattering of fire escapes, and steam rising in the streets through manhole covers. "What was it like?"

Moth starts reminiscing about some of his old haunts. He describes his two favorite clubs: Axis and Avalon; and other places: the blues bar in Cambridge, a coffee shop in Somerville, another in the North End, another called the Phoenix. He talks about the Oyster House and the Blue Ginger. He describes Gillian's and the Rat. He describes Newbury Street, with its trendy cafés, artsy boutiques, Newbury Comics – "a wicked good time," the Victor Hugo bookstore, and its posh clothing shops: Versace, Gucci, Armani.

Arturo touches the collar of his shirt. "This is Armani."

Moth's eye over the shirt. "It's nice. I like it."

Arturo looks at Moth. "Isn't that Armani?"

Moth looks down at his chest, which is looking good in Orazio's tight t-shirt. He has no idea, so he grabs the back of the shirt and pulls it out to read the tag. For some reason it doesn't surprise him that even Orazio owns Armani. "Good eye," he says.

They talk fashion as Arturo turns off the road to Pesaro, onto another road with a steady incline. Higher up into the hills, fewer buildings and more fields, a few hairpin turns, an infinite stretch of blue sky. Moth has had this conversation before, but never with a good-looking Italian man. What is it about Arturo that intrigues him so? Italy is full of beautiful men, many of them prettier than Arturo and a lot less straight. Like Juan's friend, the bartender, who is a nice piece of eye candy. *Too bad he's too young,* Moth thinks, then flips the thought around: *Too bad I'm too old.* Nothing made him feel older than a pretty teenage boy, reminding him of what he used to be, reminding him of how close he was to thirty.

Through another hill town with another beautiful church and then the road declines. "Almost there," Arturo announces. "It's about ten minutes from here."

Moth lights another cigarette. "Do you know where we're going, exactly?"

"We'll find it," the paralegal says confidently.

Moth hums.

Continuing down the road, Arturo points out a cinema. "They just play porn movies."

"Been there, have you?" Moth teases.

Arturo shoots him a look. "No," he says. Then, "Just part of the tour."

Moth smiles. Arturo does have a sense of humor. "Anything else of interest on this tour?"

Arturo shrugs. "Probably not. You'd need to come down at night, when things get interesting – then all the prostitutes and transvestites come out."

Moth wants to ask Arturo if he's been with a prostitute, or a transvestite for that matter, but instead he says, "So I've heard."

Up the road, they enter into Riccione proper. Arturo pulls up in front of a coffee bar and parks. "Let me get some directions. I'll be right back."

Moth stretches out his legs inside the car, watching Arturo walk into the café. Little does he know that in another, similar bar about ten kilometers up the road, Orazio is standing in the back of the room with the phone cradled against his shoulder, a cigarette in his other hand, his blue eyes darting around the bar as the line rings and rings. Orazio swears and puts the phone down. He grabs the phone card as it pops back out and slides it into his wallet.

He walks back to a small table against the wall where two men are sitting. At the same time, they say, "Well?"

"No answer," Orazio tells them.

The man with the long, dark ponytail says, "So, now what?"

The other man with short hair and a gold hoop in one ear speaks up. "I know a guy we can try."

"I don't know," Orazio says. He doesn't know the guy with the earring, Valentino, very well. Except that – other than Juan – Valentino is the only person he knows who has a car, and who would be willing to run this kind of errand. "Maybe we should just wait awhile."

Valentino glances at his watch. "I don't have all day, but… whatever."

Marco, the man with the ponytail, just shrugs.

Orazio ignores the two pairs of dark eyes upon him and focuses on a bottlecap lying on the table in front of him. He fiddles with it, half-wondering how long the wait for his usual dealer is going to be, half-wondering why he bothers with Valentino, when there's something about the Sicilian that he doesn't like. Better if Moth had been around. He wouldn't have minded if Moth had come along with them, lighten things up a bit. He likes Moth, trusts him, even. For not the first time he remembers how Moth read that poem last night, how his voice just rolled through Orazio and reverberated somewhere inside him, striking some chord he usually left ignored.

Little does Orazio know that Moth is only ten kilometers down the road from him, caught up in his own adventure, watching Arturo start up the car while saying he knows where they're going.

"Then let's go," Moth says.

~

Sam passes the afternoon in the back room of Basili's with Lisa, drinking tea and talking. At a certain point he tells her that he ought to go home and study for awhile, although what he really means is that he ought to go home and wait for his brother to get back from Rimini, hopefully bearing good tidings and joy. They're a little low on joy right now. Orazio had sold off most of what they had left in order to amass money for this trip.

Outside in the square he sees Juan talking with one of his friends. Sam waves from the steps, and Juan gestures him over, smiling fondly at the young man. They greet each other, exchanging kisses on both cheeks.

"You know Sergio," the Spaniard says.

"Yeah, sure," Sam says. "You're a friend of Valentino's."

"More like Valentino's fiancé," Juan says.

The Sicilian smiles. "That might be exaggerating," he says softly.

Juan slaps his hand down on Sam's shoulder. "So, what are you up to?"

Sam tells him.

"And later?"

Sam shrugs.

"Party?" Juan suggests.

"Where at?"

"My house."

Sam thinks. "Who's invited?"

"Whoever you want."

Sam thinks again. "Can I bring Moth?"

The Sicilian's elegant eyebrow rises. "Moth?" he asks, an amused look about him.

Juan looks at Sergio. "The American," he explains.

Sergio shrugs. "I don't know him."

"He's pretty," Juan says. "Maybe twenty-four or twenty-five years old, with hair down to here, with red and black streaks in his hair, always wearing a black leather jacket." Sergio makes no sign of recognition. "Hangs out at The Dive," Juan adds.

"Hmm," Sergio says. "I don't know him."

Juan sighs. "Maybe that's just as well," he says. "Older men, and all that."

Sergio grasps the jibe. "Valentino's twenty-five. That's not old."

Juan smirks, his eyes flashing. "And you are, what, sixteen?"

Sergio gives Juan a look all dark velvet. "Eighteen," he says, although he knows that Juan knows.

Juan turns back to Sam. "Sure, bring Moth."

"What time?"

"Anytime," Juan says. "Serg – what are you doing later?"

"That depends on Valentino."

Juan's eyes light up. "Hey. Idea. Sam – you wait for Orazio and Valentino to come back, then, when you're ready, come over to my house. Serg – come with me. We can stop and rent a few movies." Juan smiles devilishly. "And pick up a bottle of tequila."

"Ooh," Sergio says. "Tequila boom boom."

"Sounds good," Sam says, shifting his bag over his shoulder, says good-bye to them, and heads home. Casting a glance at the clock in the square, he calculates the amount of time that his brother has been gone. Orazio might be back at their house now, or he might not. Sam tries not to think about it too much. Disappointment sucks.

As he approaches his house, he sees Moth sitting on the stairs, waiting. "Hey, *Farfalla*."

"Hey, Sam," Moth says, standing up. "Where's your brother?"

"He went to Rimini."

"Ah."

"He should be back soon," Sam adds, unlocking the door. "Come on up."

Inside, Sam drops his bag, while Moth drops himself onto Sam's mattress. Sam picks up an elastic, tying back his hair, a pale shadow of his brother, then sits down next to Moth. "Where have you been?"

"Nowhere." Moth doesn't want to talk about his trip with Arturo, which yielded no information whatsoever. In Riccione, they had talked to a neighbor about the murder, but the guy couldn't really help them out, so they'd gone in vain. And spending a few hours with Arturo while making an effort to be on his best behavior and not flirt hadn't exactly been a satisfying experience. They'd driven back to Urbino with less conversation than on the trip out; then Arturo had dropped Moth off at Porta Lavagine about an hour ago.

"Hey, Michele?" Sam says tentatively.

"What?"

"Don't get offended, but you kind of stink."

Moth sighs. "I left all my clothes at my brother's house. I could shower but these jeans would still stink."

"Take a pair of Orazio's," Sam says. "You've already borrowed a shirt, I see."

"True." Moth reaches up to touch the fabric. "Do you think he'd mind?"

"Who, Mr. Control?" Sam asks. "He probably won't even notice when he gets back here."

Something occurs to Moth. "Are you out of junk already?"

"Yeah, since this morning. Planning ahead isn't exactly Orazio's forte."

"Well, would you like a *schizzata*?" Moth asks, Italian slang for a small shot.

"You're holding?"

"I have a little, yeah."

"Ah… I'd owe you one. Pay you back tonight."

Moth stands up. "Don't worry about it." He goes into the bedroom to get his stash, and the rest of the gear. He doesn't feel the physical need for it, but he's half in love with the idea of it. The two of them sit on the floor of the living room, preparing. Sam carefully unfolds the cigarette box foil, exposing the junk, pale on the paper.

"How much?" Sam asks.

Moth eyes the paper. "All of it."

Sam nods approvingly. "This will be one big *schizzata*."

"I have faith in your brother," Moth says.

All said and done, the boys fall back on the bed, and smoke a cigarette. Then another cigarette, neither speaking much. At some point, Moth nods off, wakes, and nods off again. When he wakes again, Sam hands him a clean glass of water, for which he is extremely grateful. Sam sits back down, reaching for another cigarette.

"They're still not back yet," Sam says.

"What time is it?" Moth says.

"About seven-thirty."

"Well, you know how Orazio is."

"I'm not worried," Sam says, although his expression says otherwise.

Moth rises, feeling some energy coming back to him. "I'll be in the shower," he says.

In the bathroom, Moth strips down and gets under the hot spray. Soap and shampoo. He steps out, not thinking about much, drying off with the relatively clean towel he'd found. He hears voices coming from the other room, recognizing Orazio's. Moth touches his jaw and decides to shave. He finds a razor and some shaving cream on the bathroom shelf and goes about the task. He is rinsing his face when Orazio bangs on the door.

"We're waiting for you, hurry up," Orazio calls.

"Wait a minute," Moth calls back. He wraps the towel around his waist and steps out. From the bedroom doorway he spies people in the living room, drinking beers.

"About time," Orazio says.

"What's up?" Moth asks. His eyes move from one to the other. Sam, Marco, Orazio and another man he doesn't know, leaning in the doorway to the kitchen, handsome, well-dressed, perfectly groomed. His dark eyes flicker briefly over Moth, assessing, although not necessarily complimentary. Neutral.

"Nice tattoo," Marco says.

"Thanks," Moth replies automatically.

"Get dressed," Orazio orders. "We're going to Juan's."

"He's having a party," Sam adds.

"We need to pick up Davide," Marco says.

"My car only holds five," Valentino points out.

"Call him and tell him to meet us there," Orazio says.

"He doesn't know where Juan lives," Marco says.

"Then give him directions."

"Well, I don't know where Juan lives."

"Then I'll give you directions and you can give them to Davide."

"Or you could give them to Davide."

"Jesus Christ," Orazio says. "Fine. I'll call him. Give me his number."

Marco rattles off the number.

"Do you think I'm going to remember that?" Orazio complains. "Write it down."

"Oh, for fuck's sake," Marco mumbles, but writes down the phone number with pen and paper negotiated from Sam, and hands it to Orazio. Orazio stuffs the paper into his pocket. He stops in front of Moth, touching Moth's arm and whispering conspiratorially into Moth's ear. "I've got a surprise for you."

Intrigued and perplexed, Moth whispers back, "What is it?"

Orazio grins. "If I told you, it wouldn't be a surprise, would it?"

⁓

Juan lives in a one-bedroom apartment near the *colleghi*, recently renovated. After they walk through the heavy green door into the living room and strip off jackets, the first thing that Juan does is to show Moth the view. Standing on the balcony, Moth looks at the distant hills, twinkling with a myriad of lights against the dark.

"Like it?"

"It's nice," Moth says, meaning it.

Juan points off to the right. "You can't see it now, but, in the daylight, San Marino is over there. Have you been?"

"Not yet, no."

Orazio sticks his body out long enough to pass Moth one of the Heinekens they had picked up along the way. "Here."

"Grazie."

"Prego."

Juan studies Orazio's face, then Moth's. Orazio slips back inside.

"He looks like he's up to something," Juan comments.

Moth's thoughts flash briefly to the surprise Orazio had mentioned. "Oh, Orazio always looks like that."

Juan reflects for a moment. "You're right about that," he says.

Moth takes a swig of his beer, then notices Juan's empty hands. "Oh, hey, did you want a beer?"

Juan shakes his head. "I've been drinking tequila with a Sicilian. After that, there's no going back to beer."

"A Sicilian?"

"Damn!" Juan says. "You have to meet Sergio – Valentino's boyfriend."

Juan drags Moth back inside to find Sergio. Through the living room where Orazio sits with Marco and Davide, all three pinned in pupil. In the kitchen, at a table with two chairs, the Sicilians are drinking tequila. A stereo on the counter provides background music: GiGi D'Agostino, very upbeat. Juan introduces Moth to Sergio.

"Ah," Sergio says, offering his hand. "The American."

"Uh," Moth stutters. What an unbelievably beautiful boy, with long black coils of hair, dark eyes with thick lashes, perfect brows, and thick lips, and beautiful hands. "In a manner of speaking."

Sergio smiles. Perfect teeth, too. "Tequila?"

Moth takes the glass offered him. They toast and toss it down. It feels like fire blazing through his chest, a burst of Hell.

Juan grins in Moth's direction. "You've got to hear this story," he says. He looks at the two Sicilians. "Would you tell Moth the story?"

Valentino makes a flippant gesture. "It's not much of a story."

"Short version, then."

Moth's eye falls back on Sergio. The Sicilian gestures with the bottle, so Moth sets his glass down on the table, watching him pour another shot.

"Tell it if you want," Valentino says.

"Serg – tell Moth how old you are."

Sergio smiles at Moth. "I'm eighteen," he says.

"Tell him how long you've been with Valentino."

Those velvet eyes linger on Moth's face. "I've been with Valentino for five years."

"Five years in secret," Valentino adds, his tone implying his displeasure.

Still looking at Moth, Sergio says, "Our families would never understand. Some people down in Sicily are still a bit traditional in their thinking. Especially my father. So they don't know."

"I know what you mean," Moth says.

Sergio continues. "I met Valentino when I was thirteen years old. He was a friend of my cousin." The boy smiles softly. "He was twenty years old at the time. He seduced me."

Thirteen! Moth makes an effort not to react, but Valentino scowls when he sees the flicker in Moth's expression. But then the Sicilian huffs a sigh into his glass, grumbling. "It wasn't as bad as it sounds."

"We were in love" Sergio says, his tone teasing. But in his eyes there is a flash of genuine emotion. "Anyway, Valentino came here to study a few years ago, after completing his military service. I skipped mine to come here last September, so we could be together. It was too difficult when he was gone. So here we are. At least until Valentino graduates and finds a job."

"What kind of job?" Moth asks.

"In a bank, preferably," Valentino says.

Sam leans into the kitchen. "Hey, *Farfalla*, want to watch *Trainspotting*?"

"Sure," Moth says. He drops the shot of tequila and then follows Sam into Juan's bedroom. There are two twin beds on opposite sides of the room. Juan's friend, the bartender from Basili, sits on one.

Juan, having followed them in, sits in a chair near the television. The bartender's eye flickers over to Moth.

"Hey, how's it going?" Moth says.

"All right," the boy replies frostily.

Moth then sits on the empty bed. Sam takes the floor. They watch the movie a bit before Davide sticks his head in. "How can you watch this shit? You know, it's just going to make you want to shoot up."

"Well," Moth says. "Shooting up is always a possibility."

"Yeah, whatever," Davide says, and disappears.

"He does have a point," Sam admits.

The images on the screen are enticing. "Yeah, he does."

Orazio appears in the doorway then sits beside Moth. "Hey."

"Hey," Moth says.

The bartender gives Orazio a cold look, which Moth must remember to ask about later. Then he feels Orazio's hand in his hair, playing with it. "I like you hair," Orazio says. "Very American."

"I think it's very boring," the bartender says. "Punk hair. How 1980s."

Juan looks over. "Play nice, Dominik."

"If you want to be bold, you have to do something like this," Dominik replies, sticking out his tongue, a flash of silver stud. He catches it between his teeth, the click of metal on enamel.

Without saying a word, Moth lifts up his own shirt to expose the piercing in his left nipple. Then he drops the shirt back down, taking another sip of beer.

Juan raises an eyebrow. "That was interesting. You gentlemen have anything else to share?"

Orazio smiles his charmingly boyish smile, totally pleased about something. "I do. A surprise for Moth."

"Intriguing," Juan says.

Funny, Moth thinks, *that's what I was thinking.*

Orazio slips something out of his boot and holds it up in front of Moth. A loaded syringe, shiny and new.

"A shot?" Moth says.

"A speedball," Orazio says slowly. "We scored some coke from Valentino's friend." He checks his friend's face for a reaction. "Well?"

Moth takes the syringe from Orazio. "You are so good to me."

Juan shakes his head. "My house is not your shooting gallery."

"Jesus, Juan," Orazio says. "I've got some for you, if you'd like."

"No, thanks," Juan says. For a moment he stares at them: Moth, Orazio, and the syringe. Then he relents. "Just promise you won't OD in my bedroom."

"He won't OD," Orazio says with saintly sincerity.

"Fine, then," Juan says. "Go ahead."

Moth shifts on the bed, studying the syringe with its bright orange cap and its vaguely murky contents. Everyone is quiet, watching him. He realizes that he doesn't care; he wants it that badly. He has had a speedball before, years ago, and it was fantastic. He flicks the cap off to see the glint of a sharp, new needle, like a promise.

Then Dominik's voice comes, subdued, from the other bed. "I'll have some."

Moth feels the attention shift off him, even though his eye remains focused on the needle. Orazio's voice, with an edge, is forceful enough to stir the tendrils of Moth's *how 1980s* hair: "You're joking."

Then Dominik's voice, seemingly unperturbed. "I'll take whatever you were going to give to Juan."

"That was for *Juan*." Big stress on Juan. "What makes you think that I would give it to *you?*"

Instinctively, Moth doesn't slap his arm to raise a vein. He quietly rubs the obvious one in the crook of the elbow, already visible below the skin.

"Well, what's the difference?" Dominik says.

A hush. Needle in.

"Well, you're just a week-end chippie, anyway," Orazio says.

"Duh, it's the week-end," Dominik shoots back.

Plunger being pressed. Heart in throat, not beating.

"I've got an idea," Juan says.

Moth's body turns to jelly. He hisses out, "*Ahhhh yessss*." His heart bounds around fiercely from the coke, his limbs liquid lead from the heroin, his body full of the strangest sensations, but so fine. Attention back on him again. He leans back against the wall, half there, half gone. Juan's voice floats over him, half-registered.

"Orazio will give you my share, but on one condition," Juan says.

A pause. "Which is?" Dominik asks.

"On the condition that you suck Moth's cock," Juan says.

Orazio and Sam both snicker.

Moth half-registers the look on Dominik's face, more pissed off than anything.

"In front of everyone," Juan adds.

The snickers turn into serious laughter.

"You're so disgusting," Dominik says to Juan. He eyes Moth. Moth watches his expression, so sharp and calculating. "Fine," the bartender says suddenly. "I'll do it."

The laughter stops. Perhaps the effect that he was after.

Only Juan does not seem surprised by this turn of events. He makes a graceful, sweeping gesture, as if he were a butler and Moth were a tray of canopies. "Go ahead."

Moth sits up, pushing his hair away from his face. "Don't I get a say in this?"

Juan leans forward in his chair. "Of course," he says. "But look at that boy, Michael. Don't you want him to suck you off?"

Moth looks. He half-wishes that he could think straight, make a reasonable decision, but he cannot. That would be the heroin, not the coke.

Juan's voice again. "You ever had a boy with a tongue piercing suck you?"

Moth's own tongue is thick, his body responding on its own. That would be the coke, not the heroin. Dominik's eyes on his: dark, bedroom kind of eyes, not full of disgust, but something else. "No, I haven't."

Dominik sits there, quiet, looking at Moth. Full lips, not smiling. There's something exotic about him – mixed blood, Italian and something else. Giving Moth a moody look, almost daring him.

"It's up to you," Juan says finally. "If you want to, just say yes."

Moth can't look away from the boy. "Yes," he says, and teeters up from the bed. He crosses the room and stands in front of Dominik in a moment in which no one moves, eyes upon them. Then Moth touches the boy's face as the boy places his hands at Moth's waist. The exquisite slide of the silvery silk knit against Moth's skin – Orazio's shirt. Then Dominik pulls Moth down beside him so they are sitting side by side.

Dominik lifts his hands up to Moth's smooth face, in Moth's hair, and Moth holds on to the boy's arms, the boy's strong biceps taut under a simple black shirt, thin cotton, the warmth of skin beneath. *Kiss me,* Moth thinks, *kiss me.* Then the boy's hands return to Moth's face, and he leans forward, his lips on Moth's lips. Then Dominik pulls back and pushes Moth down on the bed, climbing over Moth, kissing Moth's neck, then pulling up Moth's shirt, his mouth on Moth's chest, a tug on the nipple ring shooting an exquisite sensation through him.

Hands on belt, Moth's eyes closed as Dominik takes him into his mouth, his tongue moving expertly, swirling around him, his pleasure heightened by the movements of the metal stud.. Then Moth's eyes open briefly and he sees Orazio, watching Moth with a strange, intense expression. Moth meets his gaze for a moment, but only that, because then Orazio turns away, gesturing to Sam, and he gets up and leaves the room.

Moth closes his eyes again while Dominik works on him. Tension building, rhythm quickening, it is over faster than Moth would have liked, but the orgasm, powerful and sudden, nearly chokes him. Good thing he's lying down; otherwise he'd collapse.

Dominik picks himself up, hovering over Moth for a moment. Smiling now. "Maybe you can repay the favor sometime," he says softly, frost melted.

"Maybe I will," Moth says, half a promise.

Dominik leaves the room. It takes Moth a moment to sit up, heart still thundering. He glances at Juan, still in the chair.

"Damn!" Juan says. "You have a beautiful face when you come."

What just happened? Moth wonders, but he doesn't voice it aloud. He has no reply for Juan. The most he can do is adjust his clothes, not think about it. Standing up, he feels strange, but falsely believes that it's the drugs in his blood that are causing this feeling. His head spins, but the wall is there to support him. He has a sudden desire to breathe fresh air.

He steps out into the living room and sees Orazio on the sofa with Dominik, syringe in Orazio's hand. "It's this or nothing," Orazio is saying.

Dominik hesitates, staring at the needle. This scene in uncomfortably familiar to Moth; he's been here before, in Dominik's place.

Orazio's eyes, cold, on the boy. "If you're afraid to shoot up-"

"I'm not afraid," the boy interrupts.

"Well?"

Moth wants to tell him not to do it; he wants to stop this now, but he can't. He knows that he can't save the boy; he can't save anyone, not even himself. He watches in silence as Orazio injects the boy with what looks to be a dangerously large dose for a beginner.

Moth feels disgusted. Whether he's disgusted with Orazio, or the boy, or himself, he doesn't know. He picks up his jacket without meeting anyone's eyes and steps outside.

Outside is Sergio, leaning against the railing, smoking a cigarette and staring out into the darkness. He turns when Moth exits. Dark eyes glossy from too much tequila, skin flushed, he takes Moth in. "Everything all right?" he asks.

"No," Moth replies.

Sergio offers him a Marlboro, which Moth takes. Sergio leans forward to light it. "That's a shame," he says.

The front door opens and Orazio steps out. He looks at Moth. "What are you doing out here?"

Moth can't keep his irritation out of his tone. "What were *you* doing in there?"

Orazio understands Moth's intention. Voice snaps. "He asked for it."

"Well, there's a rule about that – you're not supposed to shoot someone up for the first time."

Orazio's jaw clenches visibly in the light from the streetlamp above them, his stare more a glare. He's never been angry at Moth before, but there's a first time for everything. "Yeah, but I don't like him," Orazio says, cold and angry. "He deserves what he gets."

An angry silence.

"Fuck it, I'm leaving," Moth says.

Orazio's brows furrow. "Where the fuck are you going?"

"For a walk," Moth says, boots already stomping down the stairs.

"Fine!" Orazio calls out after him. He has other comments that he would like to hurl at his friend's retreating back, but Sergio's presence checks his behavior. "Fucking American boy," Orazio says softly, to himself.

"Forget him," Sergio says. "Come inside and have a tequila." Then he pauses, studying Orazio more closely. "Or two, maybe."

Orazio unclenches his jaw. *Fuck Moth.* "Yeah, sure."

Moth starts walking down through the apartment complex, huddling deeper in his jacket against the chill of the night. His head still fogged with confusion and anger, he reaches the street.

To his left is the way back to the city center, to his right *Here There Be Dragons.* He doesn't want to go back to town, there's no point in that, nowhere to go. Something buried deep within him is urging him away from others, to find a place to be alone before something terrible happens. He stands between the open gates of the complex, eyes fixed on the tree-lined road curving off into the darkness, beckoning him like a Siren, calling to that buried thing within him, with no human voices to wake him. But Moth isn't thinking of his hero, T.S. Eliot; he is recalling a more popular line by Frost:

"A road diverged in the woods and I,

I took the road less traveled by."

The dragons it is, then. He turns and heads away from the town.

He doesn't feel his body, coke and heroin numbed; the ground is only vaguely under his feet, unsteady and slippery, giving him the strange sensation that, at any moment, God is going to pull the rug out from under him, sending him flying face down to the asphalt, or to Hell.

Like most atheists, Moth thinks a lot about God, though he blames such random religious interjections on a harsh Catholic school upbringing. He used to have a favorite T-shirt with the words "Recovering Catholic" printed in bold black letters on it, until it, too, was lost somewhere. There's a happy memory attached to that article of clothing: he'd worn it on his first date with Quentin, having agreed to meet at the Au Bon Pain in Harvard Square for coffee, and upon seeing it, Quentin gave a little smile, which Moth found so attractive and which would become familiar to him in the years to come, a subtle smile that signified amusement. It had soon become a personal crusade of Moth's to often produce this particular smile of his lover's.

But Moth is not thinking about Quentin now, nor is he thinking about the connection between religion, Marx, opiates, and recovery which has manifested itself bodily in him, the void created by lack of religion now filled with junk. Instead, random thoughts and emotions dart in and out, like wasps puncturing his brain, overlaid by that glaze of indefinable anger, but an anger which is distant, muted by the junk. Orazio's face flashes before his eyes. Moth had never seen Orazio angry before, and in the younger man's face there had been an intensity that was both threatening and frightening. There was a depth of rage in Orazio of which Moth had been blissfully unaware. Moth realizes that it could have come to blows, but for what? For a criticism that Moth had made? Surely there was more to it. Orazio had an obvious dislike of Dominik. It was possible that letting Dominik blow him had been a sort of betrayal. But these thoughts are vague and incomplete. Moments frozen like photographs.

Flash: Orazio's face. Flash: Dominik kissing his mouth. Flash: the inside of the espresso cup. Flash: the dark glimmer in the Spaniard's eye. Flash: Arturo crossing the parking lot. Flash: Sam, head tossed back, mouth open with laughter. Flash: his brother's fist, striking. Flash: the Stranger penetrating him against the wall in Rat's Alley with the sensation of something hot and spiked uncurling within Moth's guts before a piercing thrust of pain.

Moth stumbles, the breath knocked out of him as though he'd been dealt a physical blow in the stomach. He manages to break his fall by seizing a tree. Rough bark scratches against his face as he gasps for air. *What the fuck?*

In clear, crisp detail, the memories of that night with the Stranger come flooding back. He remembers now, can't stop the memories. He feels a burning in his stomach, waves of nausea. Still clinging to the tree, he vomits over the grass. His face is suffused with blood, hot-- burning also in his bowels, where the Stranger stabbed him.

A sudden moment of clarity brings everything in his present into focus. He sees himself entwined with a tree on the side of a dark, twisting, empty road, in the rolling hills, the silent moon mocking him. *This is not good.*

Farther away from the road, he spies what appears to be a run-down building: crumbling stone, roof spitting out red tiles which lay broken on the ground, doors half-torn off their hinges, probably abandoned.

An inner voice speaks to him: *Go there,* it says.

He goes, approaches carefully, finds that it is indeed abandoned. Slipping through the battered hanging door, he smells a mixture of rust, damp stone, rotten hay and mildew. His pinned eyes have trouble adjusting to the dim light of the old farmhouse.

As sudden as the lucidity struck him, a blast of heat assaults him, intense and unbearable, causing him to cry out an unintelligible tangle of language. Flesh on fire, Moth claws at his clothing, dropping first jacket, shirt, then pants, until he is standing naked in the middle of the abandoned farmhouse, confused and frightened, believing that he is dying, that this is the end of him.

It is the end of him. The conscious thing which is called Michael Gallo is now usurped by the inner voice, by the dark buried thing within him. Moth's mind recoils and recedes from the ancient evil which has been biding its time, growing and infesting and spreading like a cancer throughout his body. From Moth's skin, fine, silken hairs begin to sprout, winding their way around him, collecting leaves, twigs, hay and other debris from the stone floor among their strands as they spin themselves around his body, now curled up in a fetal position on the ground, encasing him from head to toe, following their own predestined pathways, thicker and thicker, until the uninhabited shell of Moth is completely covered, obscured.

The process takes several hours to complete, but, once completed, there is an inside and an outside to the sack of hair and debris, which is starting to harden, turning brown, glossy and smooth. Inside there is a man, curled up as a fetus in a womb, waiting to be born.

Outside is a hardening sack, egg-shaped, unlike any lepidopterist has ever seen among butterflies and moths in the natural world, but which appears to be, indisputably, a cocoon.

EIGHT

Arturo sits in Basili's, with the newspaper open. He orders a glass of juice from the waitress when she comes to his table. He then shrugs off his jacket and checks the time on his cell phone. Chiara is late, but that doesn't surprise him. She had agreed to meet him after her faculty meeting, but those meetings generally run late, and Chiara tends to get caught up in conversations with colleagues once she starts chatting, which takes her a long time to stop. Arturo returns the phone to his jacket pocket and returns his attention to the newspaper.

He consciously avoids scanning the news for anything related to gold-eyed killers. *Enough is enough.* Enough trying to make faulty connections based on circumstantial evidence, enough with keeping company with gay drug addicts. Having reached a dead end in Riccione, they were out of leads. There was no where else to go. Also, the last thing Arturo needs is to be associated with a guy like Moth. Urbino is a small town, everyone knows each other, and everyone is always watching. If people found out that he was spending time with Luciano's brother, Arturo would be the one to suffer the consequences of gossip and ribbing from his friends. Considering the situation more carefully, last night he realized that such gossip could be detrimental to Chiara's career, and he knew he would not be able to forgive himself if he put her in a position of *brutta figura*. Appearances were everything.

He knows how to play the game – his reputation is untarnished. Growing up, he had behaved as the perfect son, never getting into trouble, never using drugs. He studied and got high marks, took care of his aging parents, even stayed in Urbino to attend university in order to remain close to them. There he worked hard, putting in long hours in the law section of the library on his thesis and graduated with honors. Now he is doing his *pratica* with Luciano.

He should forget all this craziness and return to his studies. He has exams to take, one to allow him to practice law, the other to teach. He knows he will pass. His future is laid out before him and it is a rosy picture. He will become a lawyer, buy a house, and marry Chiara. They'll have enough money to buy a beautiful house, a car better than his Fiat, maybe get a dog, and be able to travel once a year to all those hot climate vacation places he and Chiara had talked about. A perfect, enviable life.

He stops perusing the sports section when his best friend Stefano drops by his table. Stefano also has an enviable life, works in his father's company full-time now that he finished his degree in sociology, though the degree was unnecessary as Stefano's guaranteed not only a good living, but also a house his parents had built for him on the outskirts of town, now empty, waiting for the moment Stefano will marry his long-time girlfriend Sofia and move in. But Arturo can't envy his friend the silver spoon he was born with. Stefano, too, had studied hard, also graduating with honors, as if to prove that he was willing to work hard, too, and was able to accomplish his goals all on his own.

Despite his insistence that he has to leave, Stefano lingers to talk with Arturo for nearly ten minutes. They haven't seen each other in a few days, but Stefano has much to tell him, including an amusing story about how one their friends drank too much at a dinner the night before and made a fool of himself trying to flirt with a pretty German tourist who spoke no Italian. Arturo laughs, wishing he'd been present.

Arturo has less to share but mentions Chiara's mother's sprained ankle, for which Stefano expresses his condolences, and then they shift into a discussion of soccer. Arturo's team, Torino, is slotted to play Reggio Calabria tomorrow, so Stefano invites him over to watch the game, naming the friends who've already agreed to come. The issue settled, Stefano takes his leave, making a gesture – pinkie and thumb extended – for Arturo to call him later, and Arturo watches his friend saunter out the door.

He picks up the glass that the waitress had delivered during his conversation with Stefano. He drinks from it. It is already half-empty. Or perhaps it is half-full. At any rate, it reminds him that he's still waiting for Chiara, so he takes his cell phone out of his pocket to check the time. As he looks at the screen, it flashes at him, ringing. He stares at the unfamiliar number. Slightly annoyed, Arturo presses the button and places the phone to his ear.

"*Pronto? Chi è?*"

After a brief pause, a voice responds. "Is this the guy who was looking for information yesterday about the murder in Riccione?"

Arturo does not immediately reply, debating. The list of pros and cons for his every possible response flash on a big blackboard in his brain. His mind scans through all of them, lingering on each reaction, reassessing and rejecting each one in turn. The entire process takes a split second. "Yes," he admits, still curious, and sees no immediate harm in talking to the person on the other end. "Who is this?"

"Listen," the caller says. "What's your interest in this? Are you a cop?"

"No, I'm not a cop. My interest in this is personal."

The caller hesitates again. "Excuse me if I sound rude, but what the hell does that mean?"

Arturo bristles, then glances around the bar to see if anyone is listening to his half of this bizarre exchange. No one pays him any attention. "Listen, I don't know who you are, but you called me. Why?"

"Maybe it was a bad idea," the caller says.

Arturo half-expects the man to hang up, but the line remains open. He suspects that this guy knows something, and he wants to talk about it; otherwise, he wouldn't have called. Arturo decides to stretch the truth and says, "Okay, a guy was killed in Urbino a couple of days ago. I know someone there who saw the killer. We think it might have been the same guy."

A long silence. "What makes you think that?" the caller asks.

Arturo lowers his voice. "How many guys with gold-colored eyes do you think there are running around killing people?" There is no response. "Listen, this whole thing is crazy," Arturo says. "Do you have some information for me or not? Who are you, anyway?"

The caller makes a noise, half laugh, half grunt. "Yeah, crazy is the right word. I've got some information for you, but it's too crazy to believe."

"Trust me, if it *weren't* crazy, I probably wouldn't believe you."

The caller's voice drops down to almost unintelligible whisper. "All right, then, I'll tell you what I know." Arturo has to stick his finger in his uncovered ear in order to hear what the man is saying. "My name is Andrea Demarco. Giulio was my brother."

Giulio Demarco was the name of the kid killed in Riccione. "Go on," Arturo says, but the silence is so long that Arturo wonders if the connection has been broken. Concerned and excited, Arturo presses. "*Pronto? Pronto?* Are you still there?"

"I'm still here," Andrea says. "Listen, I think it would be better if we talked about this in person. Could we meet?"

Arturo makes another split-second decision. "When?"

"Tomorrow afternoon. Around one."

At one, Arturo would be watching the game with the guys. "Afternoon's no good. What about tomorrow morning?"

"I have to work," Andrea says. "How about in the evening, around six?"

Arturo considers. Chiara would think that he was still with his friends, and he could make up some excuse to his friends, that he had to run some errands for his parents before the shops closed. He agrees to the time and the bar Andrea suggests, a popular place on the Rimini strip whose name Arturo recognizes. Before anything further can be said, Chiara walks through the door, spots him and waves. Arturo quickly ends the call, slipping the phone in his pocket as he stands up to kiss her.

"Sorry I'm late. I got cornered by Colli," she says, dropping her briefcase and sitting down. "God, that man never stops talking." She tosses a loose lock of hair out of her eyes, smiling apologetically at him. Underneath, she is bubbling with the energy of some splendid secret. "Speaking of talking, you were probably talking to your mistress, telling her what a bad girlfriend I am, and that she should rush over and take my place," she says, an old joke of hers, half to tease, but also half hopeful to hear his denial.

"Eh?" Arturo says. "No, I was just talking to Stefano." *Well, it isn't a total lie,* he tells himself, but he feels a twinge of guilt. "He invited me over to watch the game tomorrow."

"Good, I'll be glad to get rid of you."

"You will?"

Chiara smiles. "It will give me time to prepare the big and important conference I have to give on Wednesday in Milan."

Arturo pretends hurt. "You would leave me for a big and important conference in Milan?"

"Just for a few days," she says, attempting to look sorry but excitement oozes out of her pores. "But it's very big."

"How big?"

"Huge."

He smiles and congratulates her, and she reveals the details, such as how the conference planners needed to replace a distinguished professor from Harvard who canceled at the last minute. He likes to see her so happy, her face all lit up. He sits and nods as she talks on and on. Finally she stops and laughs at herself. "God, I'm sorry, I'm rambling again, aren't I?"

Arturo shrugs, noncommittal. Then he says, "Maybe a little."

She squeezes his hand on top of the table. "Poor Arturo," she says. "Your girlfriend is going to desert you to spend almost an entire week with a bunch of stodgy old boring professors and psychologists talking about mental illness. What are you going to do without me?"

Arturo squeezes back. "You know, what I usually do when you're gone: get up, go to work, visit my parents, and then go home to study and watch TV at home alone while eating a lot of take-out pizza."

"Sounds exciting," Chiara says.

He replies with the same mock-serious tone, "More excitement than one man can handle. In fact, it might possibly kill me. I have a weak heart."

She laughs, as expected.

Life is perfect.

~

Night falls.

The moon casts its glow down upon the dusty pale stone of Urbino, perching, as it has for centuries, on its slope among the hills and woods of Le Marche. If a plane were to pass overhead and its passengers were to gaze down, they would see the little city, seemingly nestled among the rolling landscape like a jewel in a dark velvet box.

The same moon about which Leopardi – also a native of Le Marche – waxed poetic, now makes its solitary trip across the sky, shifting shadow onto stone, hill, tree and man alike. Orazio does not see the light of the moon. He is deep in the bowels of The Dive, his back against the door of the bathroom stall.

He is inside the stall. There are people outside the stall, talking loudly over the music that pulsates through the walls, but they are not waiting for him. He is aware of their presence, but he does not let himself be distracted from the task at hand, which is to feed his addiction, the syringe delicately and expertly balanced between his fingers, the hunger burning a hole in his guts. Holding his breath, Orazio jabs the needle in fiercely. Beyond the door, shrill laughter. Withdrawing the slender wick of steel, Orazio absentmindedly wipes away the bead of blood that forms on his arm, bright like a ruby on a sheet of pale velvet. Beyond the door, more laughter, but Orazio thinks nothing of it. He is beyond such triviality. He is outside of himself, outside of everything.

~

In the woods, inside the distant crumbling farmhouse, the cocoon remains undisturbed in shadow. Within the glossy casing, the coil of a man still like a frozen embryo. Moth is a man in stasis, neither alive nor dead, neither here nor elsewhere. Consciousness has fled, yet the mind continues to function, neurons firing random messages, the residue of a man's memories. One after another, often overlapping, the images flow together, forming a distorted and surreal dream. The chill of the Boston winter cutting his face as he runs. The unyielding concrete below his feet, the air like knives in his smoker's lungs, though he keeps running. Behind him, his pursuer hurls angry words at his back, threats which are only empty if Moth manages to escape.

In his memory, Moth careens around the corner, nearly running into an old woman walking her dog, and keeps running. Squeezing the stolen bag of junk harder into his sweating palm, Moth keeps running, knowing that if the pusher catches him, he'll be completely fucked. He has no time to consider the foolishness of what he's done by grabbing the junk and running, but the need had been too great, driving him to take the risk of theft. He dives into a doorway, dark enough to conceal him, gulping air which does nothing to alleviate the fire in his chest. Then he turns—

—over in the bed, opening his eyes. The room is warm, and soft light is coming through the cracks of the dusty blinds. He sees Quentin, who is slipping into a robe of dark blue terrycloth. Unaware that Moth is awake, Quentin continues through the motions. Moth watches as one long, slender arm is pushed through the loose sleeve, then the robe unfurls as Quentin reaches for the other sleeve. Suddenly stunned by the image of Quentin's body, slender and marble-white against the dark of the cloth, with the white wall behind him, Moth feels overwhelmed by the love he feels for this man. His heart, his whole being, aches with love, to the point where he is uncertain that he has the strength to even bear it. Although Moth would never admit it aloud, not even via poetry, this is the most beautiful thing that he has even seen: his lover, in a completely unguarded moment, caught in the middle of such a simple and mundane act as putting on a robe. Moth does not move for fear of breaking the spell. Quentin gathers the robe about him, his elegant hands knot the belt, and then reaches up to free the hair caught in his collar. With one graceful sweep, thick black waves break loose and swing up before cascading down his back, and as the waves crash, he sees Moth watching him, and, by smiling, ends the moment. Then he says—

—that he'll pay whatever price Moth thinks fair. Not quite sober, Moth blinks a few times, trying to absorb the meaning behind the man's words.

He looks at the man, a perfect stranger really, sitting in the restaurant across from him, twice Moth's age but not unattractive enough to have prompted Moth to refuse the invitation to dinner after they'd started chatting quite casually after a few rounds of blackjack at the same table in the Luxor casino.

The weight of the man's hand on top of Moth's is suddenly oppressive, Moth withdraws his arm back across the table as though he had been burned. Moth's lips move, forming a question to which he doesn't want to hear the answer. Before that, the man had lightly suggested the possibility of Moth coming to his room. In his youthful ignorance, the over-dinner banter had seemed like harmless flirting, but with the offer of money, everything had suddenly taken on an ugly and cheap tarnish. The man repeats his offer, adding, in a smarmy tone, "With a mouth like that, I bet you can really suck cock."

Moth feels shamed and helpless, with only the kernel of indignation that will bloom later. Later he'll wish that he had thrown his drink in the man's face, that he had caused a scene, that he had, at least, defended himself by raging to the man that he wasn't a fucking rent boy; instead, his face burning, Moth excuses himself to go to the bathroom, which he knows is near the entrance. He crosses the restaurant, pushes open the door, and steps outside, into the dark illuminated solely by the moon.

~

Inside the stall of The Dive, Orazio leans against the door with his eyes closed. Beyond the door, he hears someone say, "What the fuck is that?"

Laughter. Someone else says, "Calm the fuck down. It's just a moth."

Orazio opens his eyes and rolls them up toward the ceiling. He sees the insect fluttering above him, just out of reach. He stares at the creature as it continues on its trajectory towards the light bulb hanging over the stall. He observes without flinching as the moth crashes blindly into the light, fluttering all around it, its movements becoming more violent and desperate.

Self-destruction, Orazio thinks, but it is a hazy thought, not connected to anything at work in his conscious mind. Suddenly he has a strong desire to get out of the shit-splattered stall. He shoves the stall door open, accidentally bumping a young man with bleached hair who shouts in protest.

Orazio pauses, giving the offended boy a chance to start something. The boy glares but doesn't say anything. Orazio turns to leave, but, before he reaches the door leading out, he hears snickering, and someone, perhaps the bleached hair boy, murmurs what sounds to Orazio like, "Fucking piece of shit junkie."

A surge of fire white rage wells from the pit of his stomach up to the caustic bile in his throat, beyond Orazio's control. Moving fast, he spins, attacking the boy with rapid blows. No stranger to fighting, Orazio has learned that if a man is small, he must fight in a certain manner, striking first, fast, hard, and unrelenting until the foe has fallen. The boy is drunk and unsuspecting, his friends confused into inaction. He punches the boy again and again, blood splattering on his fist before one of the friends steps in, taking a swing at Orazio. The scene becomes a blur of confusion and chaos, but Orazio is focused, and continues to pummel the boy until someone grabs him from behind, dragging him, writhing and kicking, out of the bathrooms, and somehow up the stairs and into the alley.

Orazio finally pulls free, whirling around to see who had grabbed him. It is Juan, out of breath, his hair ruffled. With an expression of exasperation, Juan growls at him.

"Shit, Orazio, get the fuck out of here before someone calls the cops."

Orazio feels the throb in his right hand from where he had punched the guy in the mouth. However, his anger is already dissipating. He doubts that any of those bastards in the club would personally invite the police down on all their asses, but he doesn't want to hang around any longer. "Yeah, whatever," he mutters, stuffing his hands into the pockets of his leather jacket and heading off.

"And don't come back here tonight!" the Spaniard shouts at Orazio's back. "Unless you like full body cavity searches!"

Without stopping, Orazio removes his left hand from his pocket, and gives Juan the finger.

Juan shakes his head to himself. "Same to you," he calls out, wondering why he bothered trying to help. "Someday you'll rot in hell, my friend!"

Orazio, rage abated and energy spent, lets the words roll off him like water from glass and keeps going. But briefly he thinks, as he walks with no specific destination in mind, that perhaps he already does.

NINE

Arturo passes through the doors of *Mon Amour*, letting his eyes adjust to the dim within. Outside, the streets of Rimini are flooded with early Spring light, hinting at the promise of long summer days ahead. Fortunately, the setting sun was behind him during his drive from Urbino, but its random flash in the rear-view mirror made him wonder just where he had misplaced his sunglasses. It would be a shame if he had lost them. Faced with row upon row of frames on the walls of the *optometrista* in Pesaro's shopping center, it had taken a long time to find just the right pair, even with Chiara's input. Arturo didn't like shopping much and would rather go without the quintessential Italian accessory than submit to the ordeal of buying a new pair.

But still, the light.

His eyes adjusted, he surveys the room, looking for Andrea Demarco. He doesn't even know what the guy looks like, having overlooked this detail in his rush to hang up the phone yesterday. The bar stretches out before him, red leather booths frame a small dance floor, and, beyond that, the bar area hugs the right wall. A lone couple sits in one of the booths, drinking pale liquid from tall glasses. At the bar, a man with dark hair past his shoulders sits with a bottle of beer. A moment passes before the man looks over at Arturo, watching him curiously. Hesitantly he raises his hand and gestures Arturo to come over.

As he approaches, Arturo gets a better look at the guy. Tall and skinny, with a long face from which two rolling orbs assess Arturo in a guarded manner. Big dark eyes that are too grand for their host, giving the man a haunted look. Up close, Arturo notices that the man's face is slightly pocked. "Demarco?" Arturo says.

"Sit down," Andrea tells him. The paralegal reluctantly obeys, ordering a beer from the bartender as he glides by. After the beer arrives, they wait for the bartender to move away again. Andrea takes a cigarette and holds the pack towards Arturo, who declines with a wave of his hand. Andrea lights up, then asks, "You sure you want to hear this?"

Arturo feels annoyed. *Obviously,* since he drove all the way out here. "Yeah, I'm interested." Then a question which has been floating around his mind pops out. "How did you know I came out to Riccione the other day?"

Blowing smoke, Andrea shrugs. "I'm friends with the guy you talked to – the neighbor – and he called me after you left."

"Right."

With restless fingers, Andrea turns the cigarette pack over in his hands a few times, looking thoughtful. Arturo considers just demanding the information so he can get out of there, but decides to wait a little longer. Finally, Andrea begins to speak.

"Well," he says, not looking at Arturo, and speaks haltingly, as if he were drawing up the memories like water from a well. "All right. Let me start somewhere near the beginning. Giulio, my brother, was living with a friend of his, Daniele. A bit of a prick, but, whatever." Andrea pauses, then adds, "He was gay, by the way."

Arturo raises an eyebrow. "Who? Your brother?"

"Yeah, Daniele, too." Andrea takes a drag. "Anyway, there were always people crashing over there – 'Daniele's strays,' my brother called them. Other gay guys, mostly, he'd met at the clubs or on the beach. Giulio complained a lot, but I don't think he really cared that much." Andrea pauses again. "There is a point to all this."

"Sure," Arturo says.

"Well," Andrea continues, "so there was this one guy crashing there. His name was Cristiano. Never did learn his last name. Kind of tall and thin with really long black hair, all the way down his back. I don't know where Daniele found this guy, but Daniele had a big crush on him, then, there you have it, the guy was crashing at their place."

Arturo takes a swig of beer. "Don't tell me. This guy – Cristiano – had gold eyes."

"No," Andrea says, with a strange expression. "Not at first."

Arturo leans closer.

"Anyway, what happened next is still unclear. Afterwards, when we talked about it, we thought maybe it had something to do with the ad that Cristiano had placed in one of those papers – an ad to meet other men. But we weren't certain." Andrea pauses, studying his cigarette for a moment before continuing. "Well, one weekend, Giulio, Daniele, and I went up to Venice. Cristiano stayed behind. We left on a Wednesday and came back late on the following Sunday. We found…" Andrea stops, laughing to himself. "I still don't know what we found. It was fucking freaky. It looked like a cocoon."

"A cocoon?" Arturo asks. "You mean like a bug makes?"

"Yeah, but bigger. Really big." His restless hands make a gesture, measuring in the air an object perhaps three feet high and nearly as wide. "So, there we were, looking at it. We were debating what the fuck it was. I remember that Daniele thought it was a joke of Cristiano's. Or like an art project. At any rate, nobody wanted to touch it. It was just too weird. Then, while we were still talking about it, it opened."

At this point, Andrea meets Arturo's eyes. Arturo's initial thought is that this is a long line of bullshit. Instead of saying so, he tries to keep his expression neutral. "And then?"

"Fucking Cristiano was in it. Naked. The thing opened and he fell out of it onto the floor. You can't imagine." Andrea laughs again, this time weaker. "We picked him up and got him dressed. He seemed okay, just a little confused. Then I don't know what happened. Daniele gave me a ride home." Andrea stops, sucking harder on his cigarette. "When he came out, his eyes were yellow. At first, he said that they had always been like that, then later he said something about contact lenses. As I said, he was confused, so we didn't think too much of it."

Arturo waits.

"A couple days later I got a call. Cristiano was gone and my brother was dead."

Arturo thinks for a moment. "I'm sorry."

Andrea shrugs.

Arturo considers the story. It was crazy all right, just as crazy as the other cases he had found. But it could be the same guy regardless, it could be Moth's stranger. "I don't suppose you have a picture of this guy?"

Andrea shakes his head. "No, no pictures. When he disappeared, he left nothing behind. Even that damn cocoon, or whatever it was, was just gone. They searched the whole apartment and didn't even find a single fucking fingerprint, a single hair from his head, like he'd never even existed, gone without a trace."

~

The moon traces an arc over Urbino. Over the towers, the walls, the woods and the hills. It does not touch the cocoon hidden in the abandoned farmhouse.

Within the cocoon, the man who was Michael Gallo continues to transform. Memories continue to flicker like Morse code, rapid and broken, across the screen of his otherwise empty mind. The outer world and the inner world have become the same: he is unaware of either, they are meaningless.

The images that flash on the screen are Moth's strongest memories, the ones, if asked, he would claim had the most influence on him, the ones that shaped his character. Each event that had left an invisible scar.

Flicker. Moth is in the forest with his junky ex, listening to the silence, musing that if he could only listen hard enough, he would be able to hear the secrets whispered by the trees. It is here in this sacred green space that his ex asks him to roll up his sleeve for the third time, revealing his naked arm, not unlike drawing up a curtain to reveal a spot-lit stage. In his hand, the syringe, patient and promising like a new lover, beckoning with its murky liquid, the moonlight glint on the wire-thin needle. The second time, he'd done too much, and spent the rest of the night puking. This time, his ex has adjusted the dose that he injects into the susceptible crook of Moth's arm. His left arm, pallid between the black velvet of his sleeve and the black leather strap of the Movado watch. Then, later, lying on the grass in the park, high as mountain peaks, his ex says, *I'm only being nice to you because I'm madly in love with you.*

Flicker. …The lights dim, and the curtains rise. It was Moth's idea to invite some of his classmates to see the play. After all, since it's

Shakespeare, it's like extra credit for class, and, besides, he's learned that in *Love's Labour's Lost* there is a character named Moth. One who isn't a fairy, with friends named Cobweb, Mustardseed and Peaseblossom.

Don Adriano: How hast thou purchased this experience?

Moth: By my penny of observation.

After the play, he meets a man at a pub near Charing Cross after the show—tall, dark, and handsome as a stereotype—a stranger also named Michael. Drunk enough to make a bad decision, he follows the other Michael home. He realizes his mistake too late, only once the man is inside him, no condom, no lube even. To Moth's weak protest, the other Michael only pins him more firmly to the bed, telling him, *Shut the fuck up, you're gonna ruin it.* Moth is startled into silence. Too many pints of snakebite and bitters at the pub makes it hard to think. He tells himself that it is too late to stop, that he should just let the man finish, and then he can go the hell home. He thinks maybe he wanted to be hurt, and a small part of him thinks he might even deserve it.

Flicker. At Au Bon Pain in Harvard Square, wearing his "Recovering Catholic" t-shirt, as Quentin smiles that smile for the first time. Moth falls in love with him then, just a little. Sunlight breaks through the clouds. Moth blinks in the sudden brightness. Quentin sips from his large paper coffee cup, then nervously twists a silver Hopi ring around his middle finger. Moth glances out over Harvard Square. He randomly thinks that the Square is like a stage. And he and Quentin are merely players, strutting and fretting their way full of sound and fury to dusty death. He has purchased this experience with his penny of observation.

This memory, like all the rest, is as worthless as a penny, signifying nothing. It merely flashes on the screen, then fades away, along with Moth's humanity.

Exit the player, stage left.

Inside the cocoon, the monster kicks.

TEN

Night falls.

Arturo never imagined that he would be standing here, in front of The Dive, but here he is. Briefly he considers the circumstances that brought him here. Since his meeting with Andrea Demarco, he's been of two minds. Part of him believes that he ought to let it all go, that all of this is crazy. Hell, he'd never bought into the paranormal; he'd scoffed at even the most common of Italian superstitions, such as the evil eye. But another part thinks that he's already come this far, that he's already involved, so he shouldn't give up now.

He needs to *know.* He's hooked.

Except that there's a major monkey wrench in his otherwise perfect plan: it's Monday night. The Dive is closed.

Because he is of two minds, a part of him feels relief. The other part is a vague annoyance that his plans have been thwarted. Except... like most of the locals of his generation, he is aware of the infamy surrounding the alley behind the club, where most of Urbino's seedy transactions take place. And this is, in his opinion – which is as unkind as it is accurate – probably his best option for finding Moth.

Arturo walks around the block to the back of the club. At the entrance of the alley, he hesitates. Not that he's afraid to go in – although he does feel a twinge of discomfort, more from a concern that someone might see him rather than what he might see within. However, his hesitation is brief. Sometimes a man has to do unpleasant things in his search for truth. Steeling his nerves, he steps into the alley.

No streetlights illuminate this scene, and from the inky shadows he feels the curious gazes of the hustlers crawling over him. Searching, his own gaze meets theirs. Most of the men look back innocuously, except for one man who moves his mouth in a sort of smile – or was he blowing Arturo a kiss? *Gross*, Arturo thinks, but before he can react, he hears a click to his left: the metallic snap of a Zippo lighter being flicked, then a golden flame which suddenly illuminates a young man's face, bathing it in light, creating a Caravaggio chiaroscuro moment.

Arturo recognizes that face.

The cigarette hisses, and the Zippo snaps shut. From the dark, Orazio regards Arturo curiously, almost ruefully.

Arturo steps towards him. "Hey. You know Michele Gallo, right?"

Orazio takes a long drag, contemplating him, silent, too cool for words. Finally, he replies through a throat full of smoke. "What about him?"

"My name is –"

"I know who you are."

Great, Arturo thinks, but bites back his sarcasm. Confrontation won't get him what he wants. "You know where he is?"

Orazio shrugs. He really doesn't know where Moth is. Nor would he admit that he even cares, not after the spat they had at Juan's party. Anyway, he figured that Moth would come around eventually when he needed a fix, a place to crash, or just had a burning desire to fill Sam's head with more philosophical bullshit.

Arturo's voice is sharp-edged with impatience. "You really don't know where he is?"

Orazio's eyes narrow. He doesn't like Arturo's tone, though it does confirm his initial impression that the guy is an asshole. He's not sure why Moth has a thing for the paralegal. Sure, he's good-looking, though way too clean cut for Orazio's taste, and he does have a luscious mouth and pretty eyes. Orazio remembers Moth's poetic line about *the cool green Buddhas beckoning*, but as for Orazio, he is immune.

Orazio tilts his head as he takes another long drag off his cigarette. "Why are you so interested in Michael, anyway?" he asks coldly. "You guys going steady?"

Arturo grimaces. Somehow he resists the urge to snap back. Clearly, he's getting nowhere. "Look. If you see him, tell him..." *Tell him what?* Arturo searches for a message that implies urgency, but remains depersonalized. "Just tell him that his brother is looking for him. And probably the police, since he missed his court hearing."

"Shit," Orazio mutters automatically. "Yeah, I'll tell him."

"Thanks," Arturo says, also automatically, then turns to go.

Orazio watches Arturo walk away, thinking about Moth, and the fine mess he's gotten himself into, and on so many levels. Then again, he's too high to feel too much genuine concern. Still, the paralegal has raised a good point:

Where the fuck is Moth?

ELEVEN

This is how a monster is born:

In an abandoned farmhouse on the outskirts of Urbino, the birth pangs begin with a twitch. A crack appears in the otherworldly, almost alien, cocoon. From within, another movement – a more violent kick – expands the crack. Through the widening fissure, an arm breaks free, the hand opens, flexing as though the fingers were gasping in the very air, gulping it down. Following the arm, a shoulder, then a head capped by dark, sweat-drenched hair. Finally, all at once as if compelled by an unseen force, the rest of the body slithers out. It slumps to the damp ground with the cold, brutal crush of flesh against rough hay and broken terracotta tiles.

Dizzy and disoriented, Moth lies still for a moment, not thinking, only breathing in the mildewy air. Thinking is impossible. It isn't unlike the night in which the stranger fucked him in Rats' Alley. Weak as a newborn, he stirs slowly, testing each limb. He has just enough wherewithal to realize that he is naked, and that the clothes strewn around the floor are his. With Herculean effort, he manages to dress himself, fumbling stiff-fingered with the zippers and buttons.

He remembers nothing. There is only a spike of instinct that both curdles and heats his blood, telling him to get away, to get the fuck out. Dressed, he stumbles through the broken doors halfway off their hinges, catching his shirt – Orazio's shirt – on a stray nail. It tears a fingertip-sized hole in the fabric before Moth manages to untangle himself.

The sunlight blazes, blinding him. His knees turn to jelly and he spills to the ground, green and damp and smelling richly of soil. It takes him a moment to regain his footing, to stumble blindly forth towards the road, using tree trunks to steady his path.

At the road, he stumbles again. This time hard asphalt jars his kneecaps, scrapes the palms of his hands. An animal groan escapes his cracked lips, forced through an even drier throat. He tries to get his feet back under him, only dimly aware of the roar of an engine growing increasingly louder as it approaches.

A red Fiat Panda careens around the corner.

Straight at Moth.

Brakes screech. A moment trickles away, then there is a staccato of hostile voices, speaking a language that Moth should understand, but in his ears becomes an incomprehensible garble. His vision goes white as his consciousness teeters away from him, and then the voices grow louder, hands under his limbs, lifting him, as the world tilts and swirls viciously away.

~

Reality creeps slowly back in. Moth, in a haze, is only vaguely aware of his body, which feels like an orange that has been brutally squeezed of all its juice, and he hears a cacophony of voices. It takes a while for the haze to lift enough for him to realize where he is: in a hospital.

Moth fucking hates hospitals.

Maybe it was the smell: body fluids and antiseptics. Or maybe it was more due to Moth's general revulsion to sickness and death. At any rate, he'd avoided them to the best of his ability, feeling vaguely fortunate that he'd never suffered any major illnesses, nor even a broken bone, in his lifetime.

The owners of the red Fiat Panda, the ones who had nearly run Moth over, had been kind enough to bring him to Urbino's only hospital, located near Porta Lavagine. After a long wait in the emergency room, Moth is finally admitted into the hospital's inner sanctum, where a doctor gives him only a cursory examination and a diagnosis of dehydration. He is then handed over to a male nurse, who leads him to a reclining chair not unlike those in a dentist's office, to be hooked up to an IV. Offering his arm, Moth can't help but notice the fleeting expression of disgust on the nurse's face as he searches for a place along Moth's track-marked arm to slide the needle in.

"You just lie here and relax," the nurse commands, and Moth can hear the implied but unspoken, *you dirty junky bastard.*

Moth lies there, half-watching the slow drip of the saline solution, half-watching the doctors and nurses who bustle through the room, except for one man in a white coat, seemingly oblivious to the commotion, his gaze affixed to a computer screen displaying a game of solitaire. At least that explained the long wait in the emergency room. Moth resists the urge to tell him *black jack on the red queen.*

A little while later, the nurse returns, checks the bag, and offers Moth a coolly polite smile. "You doing okay?" *You dirty junky bastard.*

Moth is aware that he is far from okay, that okay is a million miles away from here. Although he isn't really thinking about it, he knows that something monumental and mysterious has happened to him. Paradoxically, he knows that something essential inside him has changed, yet, despite the weakness and slowly lifting brain fog, he still feels the same.

Of course he says none of this to the nurse, who, although disapproving and judgmental, is also young and somewhat handsome–another thing which Moth can't help but notice. *Kind of hot, actually.* He doesn't speak this thought aloud. Instead, he half shrugs and says, "Yeah, I'm okay."

The nurse pauses. Almost startles, in fact, and stares at Moth for a moment intensely, almost hungrily. Then, as quickly as the look came, it is wiped away with a sharp shake of his head and a hollow, dry chuckle. "Yes. Well. Good," he says. "Just a little longer, then you'll be free to go."

Strangely, Moth doesn't hear the unspoken phrase this time.

⁓

After leaving the hospital, Moth closes the distance to Porta Lavagine and then makes the slow trek up the hill to the center of town. Despite the treatment he's received, it takes him so much focused effort that he wonders if this is what being an old man feels like and, if so, Moth has no desire to grow old and decrepit. Not that, given his current lifestyle, he expects to live to a ripe old age. Then again, when he was a teenager, he'd never imagined that he'd ever make it to twenty-eight, the age he is now.

Annoyingly, the sun is still high, whitewashing the sky and filling the streets with too much light, making him wish he still had Sam's sunglasses. He can't remember what he did with them. Upon further reflection, he vaguely recalls having taken them off and leaving them at Orazio's on the night of Juan's party.

Once in the square, he looks for a familiar face. He doesn't recognize anyone. He then counts the change in his pocket, realizes that he can't even afford an espresso, but enters Basili's anyway.

Dominik is behind the bar in his stiff white shift and black apron. *Lucky for him Orazio's speedball didn't kill him,* Moth thinks as he steps up to the bar. Dominik, inscrutable, returns his greeting. Throwing caution to the wind, Moth briefly sketches out his current financial situation and his need for caffeine.

A smile ghosts over Dominik's lips. "Sure. One moment."

As Dominik moves to the espresso maker, Moth scans the room. He notices several people looking at him. The tattoo isn't showing, so it must be the hair. Urbino is a small town, so Moth is somewhat accustomed to stares, so he doesn't think too much about it.

Dominik slides a cup and saucer across the bar to him. "On the house," he says. *And I'd suck your cock again any day.*

Moth thanks him, watching Dominik glide away, amused by his own imagination. That Dominik would actually say such a thing Moth dismisses as wishful thinking. Glancing around the room again, he notices a pair of Italian girls staring at him. As his gaze alights upon them, they quickly look away, giggling and whispering. They aren't the only ones watching him.

What the fuck? Moth feels exposed and on display like one of those anatomical wax figures he'd seen once in Florence at *La Specola*. He doesn't like it. Downing the rest of his coffee, he waves farewell to Dominik then leaves the bar.

He blinks in the bright light, crosses the square to one of the pay phones. He leans against the plexiglass wall of the booth, digging a phone card out of his wallet. He wants to talk to Arturo, but doesn't have his number, so he dials Orazio's house instead.

After four rings, Orazio answers, his voice encrusted with sleep. *"Pronto? Chi è?"*

"Hey. It's Michael."

"Oh." Moth hears a crackle of movement, then the unmistakeable click of a Zippo. He can almost taste the smoke across the line. "About time you showed up, princess. Sam was worried."

Funny how unsurprising Moth finds Orazio's lack of concern. "Sorry."

"Yeah, sure. Where in the hell have you been, anyway?"

Moth considers various answers. "Nowhere."

"Whatever," Orazio grumbles. "Oh, by the way. That guy with the face of an asshole came looking for you last night. Came right into Rats' Alley. Are you hanging out with him now? Cause if so, I question your taste."

"Why? You jealous?"

Orazio snorts. "Of that guy? That's a joke. Fine, you go hang out with him all you want, but he's never gonna fuck you. You know that, right?"

Truth hurts. "Fuck you, Orazio. I'm not talking to you anymore," Moth growls into the receiver. This is the moment when he should dramatically hang up, but the truth is that he has no other friends and nowhere else to go.

Silence. Then Orazio heaves an exasperated sigh. "Just come over tonight. Sam should be back from class in a couple of hours."

A devil of a fellow, Moth thinks, but doesn't say it this time, feeling slightly irked by Orazio. "See you," he says.

⁓

A few hours later, Moth is met by Orazio at the apartment door. The younger man's face is pale and somewhat haggard. "Just so you know," he says in a low voice, a warning, "There's a *femmina* here. Followed Sam home."

Given the way Orazio says it, Moth half-expects to find a female dog or cat in the living room. But he recognizes the girl sitting on the mattress next to Sam: Lisa. Lisa from Lecce.

It still has a nice ring to it.

Greetings are exchanged, Moth leaning down for the customary air kisses. Then Sam smiles, imp-like. "*Farfalla*. Question."

Ignoring Orazio's eye-rolling, Moth considers a few questions. None of them are very good, but he settles on, "Why do they say 'cold as hell' when hell is hot?"

Sam considers this most seriously.

Orazio, hands shoved in his armpits as though *he* were cold, snorts. "Dante's hell was cold. In the tenth circle, the very center, the devil is trapped in ice, for all eternity. So 'cold as hell' makes sense in that context."

Everyone stares at him.

"What?" he snaps at them. "I did go to school, you know."

Moth clasps him consolingly on the shoulder. "You mind if I take a shower?"

Orazio shrugs. Moth reads the gesture as permission granted and retires.

In the tiny bathroom, Moth twists on the taps in the shower stall. Before the mirror steams up, he takes a deep breath and turns to confront his reflection.

He meets his own eyes in the mirror. A prickly feeling of dread chills the pit of his stomach and jags his heartbeat.

His eyes are no longer brown.

They're gold.

"Fuck me," he whispers. He stares at himself until the steam finally obscures the mirror. The sick cold feeling lingers in his stomach, icing his blood. But is he really all that surprised? An attempt at soul-searching reveals an answer in very little time. *Of course not.*

He thinks superficial thoughts under the hot spray and after, while towel-drying his hair. There is much he does not know. He knows *who* has the answers, though that person's *where* eludes him. Until he finds the Stranger, he only knows that something weird and fucked-up has happened to him.

He wraps the towel around his waist. Exits the bathroom. Finds Orazio in the bedroom, sitting at the edge of the mattress, smoking. When he offers the pack to Moth, Moth sits down beside him, accepting a Marlboro. With a gracious gesture, Orazio lights it for him, and they smoke together briefly in silence.

In the living room, the voices of the others are muted, indecipherable. Orazio pauses to stare at the burning end of his cigarette. "You know," he says gravely, "*Voglio farmi una pera.*" He pauses again, then eyes Moth. "How do you say that in English?"

"I want a fix," Moth translates loosely.

Orazio repeats the phrase in English. Thinks. Then says, "I know this word 'fix.' *Riparare* – to repair, yes? Like when something is broken."

"That's right."

Orazio tilts his head, pensive. "I like it. It's appropriate."

Moth raises an eyebrow. "So, all junkies are broken?"

"Yes," Orazio says, a statement so resolute that it permits no argument. "If they weren't broken, they wouldn't need heroin." He leans forward to stub out his cigarette. Gestures at Moth's chest. "Didn't that hurt?"

"The piercing? Yes." Moth grins. "You should get one."

"The hell I will," Orazio grumbles. "The tattoo was bad enough." He pauses, his gaze trailing over Moth's dragon. "Not like yours, of course. Yours is impressive."

Moth, still smoking, basks in the flattery, contemplates making a joke about how his is much bigger than Orazio's. Except that Orazio then replaces his gaze with his hand, fingertips lightly tracing Moth's tattoo.

The silence swells. The air is electric. The expression on Orazio's face is anything but subtle. It is lush: with parted lips, half-closed eyes, and color in the cheeks, he is the embodiment of *boy in heat.*

It's sudden and unexpected, but Moth doesn't stop Orazio from trailing his fingers up his arm and over his shoulder, following the dragon's curving spine; doesn't stop Orazio from boldly taking his cigarette and carelessly crushing it out in the ashtray; does not withdraw even when he feels Orazio's breath against his lips, moving in close for an uncharacteristically shy and fumbling sort of kiss.

Deep inside, Moth feels something unravel, the sensation indescribable – like some alien fabric, pressing up against the inside of his skin, longing for release.

Orazio sighs into Moth's mouth, then his shyness vanishes without a trace, leaving only desperate need. Fingers curl, lips devour. Moth is quickly divested of his towel and then both of them are pulling Orazio out of his clothes.

Naked, Orazio is beautiful, all hard planes and curving muscle under golden skin. Breathless, Orazio pulls back to look down at Moth, his blue eyes glittering. Only their dicks are touching, jutting out and across one another like foils at the beginning of a duel. "What do you want?"

Strange, Moth thinks distractedly, *how quick the transition from friendship to intimacy can be.* Being himself, Moth can only answer a question with a question of his own. "What do *you* want?"

Orazio's cock jumps hard, battering the air. His voice is thick. "I want you to fuck me."

The alien thing continues to uncoil, now filling him so that it hurts. But Moth is not so reckless that he's forgotten that Orazio is still a junky and a hustler. "Ahh... you have a condom?"

Nonplussed by the request, Orazio tilts his head towards the drawer in the table.

Moth scrambles out from underneath Orazio. Opens the drawer. Finds some lube as well as the condom. He tears the wrapper open with his teeth. Struggles with the condom. Fuck, he hates these damn Italian condoms. It doesn't help that Orazio is watching him with hungry interest, now supine on the bed, rearranging the pillows behind his head.

He finally manages to roll the condom on. Returns to the bed where Orazio waits, lets himself sink down between Orazio's thighs, nudging them open with his weight.

Below him, Orazio writhes in anticipation, hair snaking across the pillow, lips pulled back to reveal small, even, white teeth. The incarnation of *boy about to get fucked.* It's been a long time since Moth topped anyone, and he fumbles with the lube. Nonetheless, Orazio trembles beneath him, his breath ragged, totally lost to his need. Having this effect on the younger man makes Moth feel powerful.

Moth feels his own need, ready to spill over. Orazio isn't in the best position, but Moth decides that he can work with it. He hooks his arms under Orazio's knees, angling the boy and his cock into position. Holds. Meets Orazio's half-lidded gaze. "Are you sure?"

Orazio's reply is a strangled half-sob. "Do it. Please."

No sooner than the plea escapes Orazio's lips, the bedroom door slams open and Sam bursts in. Surprise roots him to the threshold. "What the hell...?" he begins, then shakes his head once, sharply, as if trying to dismiss the image of his brother in bed with Moth. "You guys," he says, voice thin and quivering. Come quick. It's Lisa–"

Orazio angrily pushes Moth aside. "Lisa what?"

Sam swallows hard, regains his voice. "I think she OD'd."

~

Arturo passes a pleasant evening with Stefano and two other friends, eating pizza and drinking beer at an *osteria* just outside the city limits of Urbino. The pizza is, of course, Italian, the beer Belgian, and the conversation flows, punctuated by mild ribbing and much laughter. They talk about soccer, women and politics.

"Fascists!" Francesco interjects every time someone broaches the subject of Berlusconi or Forza Italia, until Stefano tells him to shut up and drink another beer already.

Arturo, who isn't driving, has a third beer at Francesco's insistence as they linger after the meal, still speaking of important matters such as women, and also mundane matters such as work. By the time they finally spill out of the restaurant, Arturo feels slightly drunk, a Kundera-esque lightness of being, as the moon and stars suffuse his eyes – no, his very soul – with their ethereal radiance. The moment is perfect, fragile, and brief.

"I want a woman!" Francesco yells, channeling a scene from a Fellini film for no other reason than inebriation, thus ruining the moment.

Stefano locks his arm around Arturo's neck, laughing. "Come on, I'll drive you home."

Home again, Arturo has only just deposited his keys on the counter and shrugged off his leather jacket when his cell phone rings. He doesn't recognize the number. Briefly he considers ignoring it, but curiosity wins.

He is surprised to find Moth on the other end of the line. "How'd you get my number?"

"I got it from Luciano."

Arturo flops down on the sofa. "You saw your brother?"

In the background, the street noise is intensified by Moth's silence. "Yeah," he says finally, "I saw him."

Arturo bites his bottom lip, thinking. Moth probably knows the trouble he's in, then, and it's obvious that he doesn't want to talk about it. He changes the subject. "Where've you been, anyway?"

Moth ignores the question, says, "I heard you were looking for me."

"Yeah."

"Why?"

Arturo pauses, considering not revealing what he knows, and telling Moth to just forget it. But Moth is still in it just as much as he is. "I met with Andrea Demarco. The brother of the guy killed in Riccione."

Moth listens quietly at the other end of the line as Arturo briefly recounts his meeting with Demarco. Because it's not his story, Arturo presents it objectively, without judgment. These are the facts, after all. At the end of the story, he is met with more stony silence.

"Well?" Arturo prompts.

"Huh. That makes things a lot clearer."

Arturo disagrees. If anything, for him, the opposite is true. "It's crazy."

Moth laughs softly. "Yeah. Crazy is the word. Are you home?"

"Yes. Why?"

"I need a favor. Can I crash there?"

Arturo isn't expecting this. His immediate response is no, but he's too polite to refuse outright. "I don't really have room for guests."

"The couch would be fine."

"It's small. It wouldn't be comfortable."

Moth sighs. "Look. I've got nowhere else to go. I need somewhere to crash for one night. I'd just sleep in the park, but if the cops catch me, I'm screwed."

Prodded by an innate sense of decency, Arturo relents. "Fine. One night only."

~

Moth knocks on Arturo's door after a hell of an evening. First, there was the matter of Lisa's overdose. After Sam had burst in, both he and Orazio had jumped up from the bed and ran into the living room, still naked. There they found the girl, barely conscious on the mattress. Moth, unsure of what to do, hung back as Orazio started shaking her, shouting her name in her ear, and demanding that she *open her fucking eyes*, but Lisa remained unresponsive, even when Orazio resorted to a few light slaps on her face.

Moth realized then that he still wore the unused condom. Awkwardly, he peeled it off his flagging erection and, not knowing what else to do with it, tossed it aside with the intention of throwing it away later. Other than embarrassed, he was mostly grateful that Sam didn't notice. Or at least he pretended not to notice.

"Jesus Christ," Orazio muttered, then his gaze swiveled to Moth. "Help me get her up."

Moth was feeling completely useless by that point, so he was grateful to have a task. Crouching down at the girl's side, he and Orazio managed to hoist her, albeit clumsily, to her feet. After a few concerted steps with an armful of dead weight, Orazio grunted, and they returned her to the mattress.

Moth looked at Orazio. Orazio's initial calm, take-charge attitude had relieved and impressed him, but now the younger man seemed at a loss.

"We need to get her to a hospital," Moth suggested.

"Fuck," Orazio spat, then glared accusingly at Sam. "How much did you fucking give her?"

Sam gaped, guilty, speechless.

Moth grabbed Orazio's shoulder, forcing him to divert his attention from his brother. "*That* doesn't matter. What matters is that you don't want this girl dying in your goddamn living room!"

Different emotions fleeted across Orazio's face. Finally, his expression became grim. "Sam – call an ambulance," he said quietly. "And you, get out of here before the fucking cops show up."

Moth didn't argue. Instead, he went to the bedroom where he dressed quickly. With a hasty farewell, he dashed out, taking two steps at a time down the stairwell, only slowing once he was several blocks down the street.

Moth's bad night hadn't ended there. After leaving Orazio's, he'd gone to his brother's house with the intention of picking up his belongings. The reunion hadn't been pleasant, though Luciano kept his temper in check for the sake of his sleeping daughter, sparing Moth the true brunt of his anger. At least Luciano had allowed him to gather his things, including one very crucial item: his collection of colored contact lenses.

Now, it is to a blue-eyed Moth that Arturo opens the door.

"Hurry up," Arturo says as he swings the door open.

It isn't the most welcoming greeting Moth has ever had, but he's had colder. "Umm... thanks."

Arturo responds with a lilting shrug as Moth squeezes past him to sit on the same place as before, the right side of the sofa, and slides out of his jacket. "I don't suppose you have something to drink?" he asks. "Alcoholic," he clarifies, before Arturo offers him water.

Arturo checks the refrigerator. "Beer or wine."

"A beer would be great."

Arturo withdraws two bottles from the fridge, rummages through a drawer for the bottle opener, pops the tops, and then brings the bottles into the living room, handing one to Moth before he sits.

He studies his guest. There's something different about him, but Arturo can't quite put his finger on it. Then a stray thought drops into his consciousness like a bomb: *He's pretty.*

Arturo has no idea where the hell that came from and ignores it. "You didn't sound surprised when I told you about Demarco."

Moth makes a vague gesture with his free hand. "It wasn't any weirder than anything else that's happened."

"A dude crawls out of a cocoon, and you don't think that's weird?"

"I didn't say it wasn't weird. I said it wasn't any *weirder* than the other theories."

"So you don't believe it." Arturo says, as a statement, not a question.

Moth takes a slow sip of beer. "Do you?"

Arturo leans forward, elbows on knees, steepling his fingers. "I'll say this. Demarco certainly seemed to believe it."

"Ah." Moth sets the beer bottle on his knee, spinning it slowly as he thinks. "I do wonder..."

"You wonder what?"

"I wonder what sort of man a guy becomes when he emerges from a cocoon."

"A killer, apparently."

Moth is quiet for a long moment. They sip beer in silence.

"So," Moth says eventually. "Now what?"

Arturo makes that same lilting shrug. "I don't know. We're out of leads."

Silence falls again. Then Moth sighs, leaning back against the sofa as he flicks his hair back from his eyes. Licks a bit of beer foam from his lips.

He's really kind of hot, Arturo thinks and nearly chokes on his beer. He doesn't know what's gotten into him tonight. Before he can dismiss it, however, blood rushes into his face.

Moth eyes the color rising in Arturo's cheeks. He thought he'd imagined Arturo saying he was attractive, but now he's not so sure. He decides that an experiment is in order. He thinks about kissing Arturo, what it would feel like to touch him, fingers on bare skin, lips on throat, hand stroking his body. As he thinks this, Arturo's blush deepens, and he averts his gaze, staring intently at the bottle in his hand.

Moth leans forward. "Where's your girlfriend?"

Arturo sputters. "She's, uh, out of town. Conference."

Moth sets his drink on the table, takes Arturo's bottle and sets it down. Leaning closer, he places a hand on either of Arturo's knees and slowly slides his hands up Arturo's thighs.

Arturo seizes his wrists. "What are y–" he begins, indignant, but when his gaze meets Moth's, the protest dies.

Moth pushes past his resistance, hands lightly squeezing Arturo's thighs. At the same time, he leans up to press his mouth to Arturo's. All of Arturo's thoughts melt away as Moth kisses him.

His initial resistance shatters. Suddenly, he is overwhelmed by bristling, blinding need, trembling below its weight. Unthinking, he reaches up, entwining his fingers in Moth's hair, pulling Moth closer as he opens himself to the kiss. Moth's tongue tastes bitter, but Arturo scarcely notices, too focused on the feeling of his own cock, straining against his jeans. When Moth's hand grazes him through the denim, he comes harder than he's ever come before, gone, obliterated by the bomb which is the dark thing in Moth. Blind to everything but his own desperate need, he allows Moth to drag him into the bedroom and push him down, triumphant as a king who's won a war, on the bed.

TWELVE

Fingers of late morning light filter in through the bedroom blinds. From the other room, a familiar ring tone sounds, causing one figure in the bed to stir. Arms entangled in the sheets stretch, disentangle, breaking free, as the spine arches and eyelids slowly flutter open.

In the other room, the phone stops ringing.

Only half-aware, Arturo sees a pale expanse of back, crowned by a head of tousled dark hair. For a moment he mistakes the body in the bed as Chiara's. His hand reaches out automatically to stroke the bare shoulder, arriving halfway before his vision focuses and he sees the dragon tattoo. All bulging eyes and protruding tongue in full color, the dragon's face seems to mock him.

The memories come rushing back, sharp-edged and bright, like a flurry of knives toward his face. Flash: Moth's tongue in his mouth, tasting of cigarettes and beer, which he greedily sucked. Flash: the rough, unfamiliar scrape of Moth's stubble against his thighs. Flash: the sharp, blinding pain deep in his bowels, sudden and unexpected, as Moth thrust into him.

He feels a light fog in his head and a sick feeling in his stomach which he mistakes for a hangover. Worse, he can still feel a twinge of discomfort in his ass, an entirely new and unwelcome sensation.

Arturo, uncomfortable and vaguely ashamed by his nakedness, gets up in haste. He reaches for his clothes on the floor by the side of the bed. He makes no attempt to be silent, so he is pulling on his shirt when Moth wakes, shifting in the sheets.

Moth opens his eyes and sees Arturo, whose expression is grim and whose hands shake as he tugs his shirt down into place. Given Arturo's demeanor, Moth knows whatever Arturo says won't be good.

Arturo's hands curl into fists. "Get the fuck out of my house," he murmurs, adding, "Now," when Moth doesn't immediately comply.

Indignation flares in Moth's chest, unsteadying his pulse. But he throws back the sheets and picks up his clothes.

Oozing hostility, Arturo watches him dress. His anger consumes him, too much to hold. It seeps out, filling the space between them. He can't help himself, launching his next words like daggers. "If you tell anyone about this, I'll fucking kill you."

The rejection stings. At the same time, the threat scratches Moth's pride. He reacts, calculating a hurtful response. "If you're so worried about your reputation, sweetheart, then maybe you shouldn't have let me fuck you last night."

"You fucking faggot."

Moth sits down on the edge of the bed, jerking on his boots. He tosses a cool glance over his shoulder at Arturo. "Takes one to know one, doesn't it?"

At his sides, Arturo's fists quiver. He resists the urge to cross the room to pound that satisfied smirk off Moth's face. "I told you get out! And if I ever even lay eyes on you again, I'll call the cops."

The men glare at each other. The tension in the room is so thick that it would take a chainsaw to even make a dent. Moth thinks of several spiteful things he could say, but beneath Arturo's hostile acts, Moth can sense his confusion and pain.

Struck by guilt, all the desire to fight drains out of Moth. He can't bring himself to look at Arturo again as he leaves. Arturo releases the breath he didn't know he was holding when he hears the faint sound of the front door click as it closes.

~

At the law office, Arturo arrives unusually late.

In the car, he'd been debating on what he would say to Luciano, should the lawyer broach the subject of his brother. Moth is the last thing Arturo wants to talk about, so it's with no small sense of relief he finds out that Luciano is trying a case in court and won't be back until the afternoon at the earliest. Fiesta, on the other hand, has plenty of paperwork and no qualms about delegating the more mundane tasks to Arturo. Thus Arturo's morning is devoted to a stack of documents to type on Fiesta's laptop.

The task is dull and repetitive, involving a lot of cutting and pasting, which is the extent of Arturo's computer skills. Still, he's glad to have something unrelated to last night occupy his mind, yet every time he shifts in his chair, he feels that twinge of discomfort, reminding him of just how far he let Moth go.

He doesn't want to think about it, but he's too angry and ashamed to let it go. *I was drunk*, he reasons. *And that bastard took advantage.* This is a perfectly good rationalization, except, by that point, he was not drunk, nor afraid to say no.

Mostly, Arturo doesn't want to admit the truth, which is that he liked it, liked the feel of Moth's body against his. Liked the delicious tease as Moth's tongue swept over his skin. He even liked the feel of Moth's cock as Moth angled it to hit Arturo's sweet spot over and over, drawing orgasm after orgasm from him. More than liked it, he *needed* it. He probably would have begged for it if he'd still possessed the breath to do so.

He certainly doesn't want to admit that the most intense sexual experience he's ever had was with another man. How easily he'd given himself, skating dangerously out of control from the moment Moth touched him. His life, post-puberty, had been happily heterosexual until now, and he doesn't want to question his own sexuality. He doesn't need this.

The phone rings, jolting Arturo back to the present. He answers it and takes a message from the client for Luciano, meticulously writing down all the pertinent information before hanging up.

It takes him another hour to finish typing up documents. Fiesta waves him off when he announces that he's running upstairs to take a break at the bar.

Outside the law office, he walks briskly through the parking lot, hairpins up the sidewalk, then takes the stairs which lead to the bar. Other than the barista, no one is in the bar except for two lone elderly men in one corner, reading *La Gazzetta dello Sport,* the pink pages of the newspaper intermittently rustling. He skips his customary pineapple juice and orders an espresso. The television above the bar is tuned to

Rai Uno, and Arturo half watches as the espresso machine steams and rumbles to life.

On screen, a Lavazza commercial ends, and an advertisement for a show on sexual predators begins. Just the sort of sensationalist trash that the Rai's been playing a lot these days. Arturo finds this sort of television annoying, but he can't help being reminded of the first case he'd studied about the serial killer in Rimini ten years ago, the one who would pick up women in discos, take them home, have sex with them, and then kill them with a high dose of narcotics. And Chiara's question: *How did he convince all those women to go home with him?*

Last night, he'd been unable to resist Moth's advances, done things he'd never wanted to do. *Like a compulsion*, he thinks.

In Arturo's mind, something clicks.

He thinks about Moth's gold-eyed stranger, and how Moth had vanished for three days, how something about him seemed different when he returned. Another click.

He thinks about what Demarco said: *It was fucking freaky. It looked like a cocoon. When he came out, his eyes were yellow.*

Click.

He thinks about the first time Moth came to his apartment to discuss the cases with him, and Moth suggesting: *He may have been wearing contact lenses. They have all colors now. Even lenses with smiley faces on them.*

Click.

All these pieces fall together like a completed jigsaw puzzle, finally revealing its image.

"Son of a bitch," Arturo mutters under his breath, unsure of whether this is directed at Moth, at life, at the situation in general, or all three. He feels his heart pounding hard enough against his ribs that he's convinced that his heart is trying to bruise itself against the bone. Dizzy, he grips the cool marble of the bar with both hands, trying to steady his breath. *Crazy*, he thinks, but all evidence is pointing to the unbelievable.

The barista gently places the espresso cup in front of Arturo. Arturo vaguely wonders what possessed him to order something he doesn't usually drink. The second coffee this week, the last being while on the road with Moth, when, on what felt like a whim, Arturo had suggested that they stop for one. Unwittingly doing Moth's bidding.

Arturo doesn't touch the espresso right away. An innocuous white cup, with its contrasting, aromatic liquid forming a perfect circle, flecked with only the slightest hint of foam, and laden with hidden meaning.

Decided, he picks up the cup and drinks the espresso in a single swallow. It is dark and bitter and leaves a peculiar and heavy aftertaste in his mouth.

He sets the empty cup back down on the saucer, then shuffles over to the cash register at the end of the bar. There is only one piece of evidence lacking. As the barista steps up, Arturo meets his eyes, and focuses on one thought: *I don't want to pay for this coffee.*

The barista looks at Arturo for a moment with no discernible change of expression. He lifts his hand to the cash register briefly, then lets it fall again.

"On the house," he says.

~

Moth sits on a bench in the park, scrawling in his notebook, killing Arturo with his words. He should have known better than to pursue a straight guy. Those situations never ended well. And the morning-after rejection stung far more than he'd expected.

He pauses to reread what he has just written. Not satisfied with it, he crosses out the last two lines, the harsh pressure of the pen leaving its imprint through several pages. The words just aren't coming. With a sigh of frustration, he lets his gaze sweep across the park. Late afternoon light casts long shadows over the manicured green. Along the gray gravel pathway that loops around the park, there's a couple about his age, pushing a stroller. Briefly he has a *What if...?* moment. What if he weren't gay? What if he'd never done heroin? Would he have a wife now? A family? He and Quentin had talked about adopting, always at a vague distant point in the future, before their relationship turned to shit. Before the drugs. Before Moth fucked everything up.

Absentmindedly, he rubs his wrist where the watch used to be. Since the transformation, he's had no desire to shoot up, an interesting side effect, though not half as interesting as his ability to influence people into doing whatever he wants, and not even a third as interesting as that surreal sensation of something hard emerging from his cock while he fucked Arturo, followed by a release of fluid he was pretty sure wasn't semen.

At that point, Arturo choked on a gargled cry before passing out. Gravity pulled Arturo's body down to the bed, and through the tattered condom Moth glimpsed the protrusion that jutted an inch or so from the tip of his cock: sharply jagged and white like bone, still oozing milky liquid. As he stared in wonder, the bone needle retracted, nestling back inside his cock, and no amount of experimental squeezing could draw it out again.

Remembering the sharp stab of pain he'd felt while the stranger was fucking him in Rats' Alley makes everything a lot clearer.

The sun continues to dip in the sky. Moth finally gives up on his poem. He closes his little book and slips it into his jacket pocket before he follows the gravel path out of the park.

From here, there's nowhere else to go but down.

~

After work, Arturo calls Chiara. She tells him that her conference is going well. He warns her to stay away from any handsome foreign professors who might be participating, and she tells him not to worry about any of them, except for maybe that one wickedly attractive Belgian professor, and then says she misses him. Arturo echoes the sentiment, then informs her that he's been having problems with his phone battery and that she shouldn't worry if she can't reach him. This is a lie. In general, Arturo doesn't lie to Chiara. He has no secrets, and therefore no real reason to lie. Even so, the lie now comes surprisingly easy. Perhaps because he can justify it: he doesn't want her to worry.

She makes another joke about Arturo's imaginary mistress. Arturo forces a laugh. Her veiled jokes about cheating are too close to the truth to be funny anymore, but it would be suspicious if he didn't laugh.

These are Arturo's last moments as a human: faking a cheerful mood while on the phone with his girlfriend. So banal. No sooner has he hung up than the dark thing within him roars to life. He is caught in a sudden blast of fire, not unlike the time in Murano when he'd stood before the open furnace in one of the glass studios. Stubbornly, Arturo had thought that he could somehow resist the changes he now feels within him by sheer will alone. But the heat is unbearable. He barely represses a scream as he tears off his clothes. An unconscious decision made, he crawls toward the darkest part of the apartment, as fine silken hairs begin to sprout from his skin. The hairs elongate, whipping in the air like angry tentacles before coiling around his body. Unable to resist, Arturo collapses mindlessly into a fetal position in the corner of the windowless room.

~

Moth walks down the hill. In the square he scans the crowd for a familiar face. No Sam, no Orazio, no Juan, nor any of his other acquaintances, even though the square is full of people who are taking *la passeggiata*, the traditional evening stroll. He takes stock of the situation: he has no friends in view, he's broke, and he hasn't eaten all day. Overall: not good.

He'd made a point of checking the *cronaca* in the newspaper at the bar earlier in the day, searching for news of Lisa's death. He didn't find anything, but that didn't necessarily mean that she was still alive. Until he talked to one of the boys, he wouldn't know what had happened to her.

Assuming that the boys weren't in jail for possession. Or involuntary manslaughter. Anything was possible.

Ignoring his hunger, Moth crosses over to the phone booth. He tries calling Arturo, declining to leave a message when it goes to voice mail. Tucking the phone card back in his wallet, he scans the crowd again. He wishes he would run into someone he knows. He'd much rather go out for a drink – or, better yet, a meal – than the option he is currently considering, which is to head over to Arturo's apartment. He doesn't really relish the idea of talking to Arturo, and immensely dislikes the possibility of Arturo opening the door.

He also dislikes the possibility of Arturo being *unable* to open the door.

Either way, he needs to *know.*

He has no excuses, nowhere else to be, and nothing else to do. Resigned, he begins the trek to Arturo's apartment building.

From the *Piazza della Repubblica* he has to ascend the hill, up past Orazio's building, past Raphael's house – one of Urbino's few tourist attractions – then past the park and out through the *Pian del Monte.* From the wall, the road slopes down again, shops eventually giving way to a more residential area. As Moth walks, the architecture becomes more modern, clean but flavorless, a contrast to the dusty stone buildings within the city's Renaissance walls.

At Arturo's door, he rings the bell, straightens his back, and waits. When there is no response, he crouches down to check under the mat. It's a long shot, so he isn't surprised when he doesn't find a spare key. Standing up, he reaches for his wallet, extracting the phone card, which should be thin and flexible enough. He slides the corner of the card into the gap between the threshold and the door, angling it behind the latch.

It's another long shot, and not as easy as it looks in films, but with some finagling, Moth manages to pop the lock. Luck continues to be on his side because Arturo neglected to put on the chain, sparing him from having to make a bad decision about kicking the door in.

One lamp paints the living room in chiaroscuro. No one is there, although Arturo's leather jacket and keys are draped across the kitchen counter and a trail of clothes leads into the bedroom.

In the bedroom, he feels for the switch and floods the room with light. In a corner, he finds what he expected to find. He stares at it for a long time, thinking.

Then, moving cautiously, Moth approaches Arturo's cocoon.

The cocoon is large, brown and glossy, and interwoven with scraps of fabric, some of which Moth recognizes as the last shirt he'd seen Arturo wearing. He'd expected it to be papery and thin, but when he touches it, he is met with resistance, the membrane springing back against the pressure of his fingers.

I made this, Moth thinks, feeling not only proprietary but also that sense of frightening and heady anticipation of a man who is expecting his first child. He halfway expects to feel some movement, but below his touch all is still. Even so, he strangely feels closer to Arturo than he's ever felt, as though they were connected on a sub-primal level, deeper than boyhood friendship, country, or sex.

"Can you hear me, Arturo?" he ventures doubtfully, but it is possible that his voice will still arrive in Arturo's dreams, as part of the flickering memory-stream playing on the screen of his mind.

Moth makes a decision. As though wishing it farewell, Moth leans forward to press a soft, lingering kiss against the cocoon's surface.

He turns out the bedroom light, then goes into the kitchen. Raiding the refrigerator, he finds a container of leftover pasta with zucchini flowers. Once he's heated it in the microwave, he eats the leftovers standing up in the kitchen, and because he's overly conscious of being an interloper in someone else's house, he carefully washes the bowl and fork, leaving them to dry on the rack.

Finally, he turns off the living room lamp after scooping up Arturo's keys. He locks the apartment door behind him.

He still has questions. But he knows where to look for the answers.

THIRTEEN

Thursday night. Back to The Dive again. Moth stands with one foot on the curb, the other in the gutter, looking at the door of the club. Painted red, it calls to mind the image of a monstrous maw, ready to devour a victim. When he opens the door, techno music washes over him in the form of a flurry of beats battering at his skin. It steadily increases in volume as, like the poet Dante, he descends into the underworld.

Last night, after leaving Arturo's, he'd come to The Dive, looking for the Stranger. Unsuccessful, he'd eventually returned to Arturo's, where he'd slept in Arturo's bed. Inside the cocoon, all was still, though Moth suffered some strange dreams he attributed to its presence.

Now heads turn as Moth enters the club proper. He's already become accustomed to drawing stares. He's also already learned how to avoid unwanted encounters, taking his cue from Italian women: he just keeps moving, like a shark.

Now, however, he stops moving once he's reached his destination at the bar. Within a few moments, Moth allows a leech to buy him a drink. Using his power to influence others, Moth just as quickly dismisses the man.

Dozens of hungry eyes poke and prod at him as he sips his overpriced and watered-down gin and tonic. None gold.

He rattles the ice in his glass, projecting what he hopes is unavailability. He wonders where the Stranger is now, if he will come to The Dive tonight, or if he's left town. Moth frets at the latter possibility. He still wants answers that only the Stranger can give him. He doesn't even know how to define what he's become, and it wasn't like he could search the Internet to figure it out.

He is thinking about how he might allow one of the leeches currently ogling him to buy him another drink when the Stranger suddenly appears out of smoky, thin air.

It is exactly like magic. One moment there is an empty space near the dance floor, and then, a heartbeat later the stranger is filling it. In the dim light, at that distance, Moth can't discern the rim of gold iris circumscribing an enlarged pupil, but he can make out the expression of bemused annoyance, and he can see that the Stranger's gaze is fixed on him. Moth tips his glass in invitation in the Stranger's direction, then watches the Stranger's approach.

As he draws closer, Moth sees him more clearly. His appearance is startling. The hair is still long, and the body tall and lean, but all trace of the classic beauty which had captured Moth's attentions has vanished. It's a wonder that Moth even recognizes him at all – "him" without a capital "h." His looks have a conventional quality to them, neither handsome nor ugly: the mouth too full, the bones of the face too narrow, the nose too big to be truly good-looking. Only the eyes – iridescent gold in a lush of long lashes – are precisely as Moth remembers.

He's still puzzling over this change in the Stranger's appearance when the Stranger reaches him. As Moth is speechless, the Stranger speaks first, cocking a curious eyebrow at him. "I'm surprised you're still alive."

Moth doesn't know what that means, but he doesn't question it, too consumed by the need to *know*. "What the hell did you do to me?"

The Stranger does not respond. Instead he continues to regard Moth as the flashing lights pulse over them, painting their faces in reds and blues. Then his lips curl. It's not quite a smile, more an unattractive sneer. Moth feels a stab of revulsion by that ugly little smile, and it takes all his self-control to keep the disgust from showing on his face.

Someone jogs his elbow. Watery gin sloshes out of his glass, wetting his fingers. He slams the glass down on the bar, meeting the Stranger's gaze with a challenging stare. "Well?"

The smile slides off his face like ice off hot glass. The Stranger looks thoughtful, then heaves a sigh. "Let's get the hell out of here."

~

Outside the club, the Stranger turns left. Moth keeps pace with him as they briskly climb up Via Veneto. His thoughts reel, making him feel light-headed, his stomach unsettled, as though he'd just been spilled from a carnival ride. They don't speak.

Moth isn't very familiar with this section of Urbino, and soon loses his bearings as the Stranger turns right, then left, and so on, up increasingly smaller streets. The number of people they encounter also thins out until they seem to be the only two moving through Urbino. Finally, the Stranger stops before a massive wooden door with a lion's head knocker, withdrawing a set of keys. He lets Moth in and leads him up two flights of stone stairs to another door.

A switch is flipped, filling the rooms, a dining room and a sitting room, with soft light. In a glance, Moth takes in antique furniture, green glass, Persian rugs, walls filled with modern art in ornate frames. The rooms are small, but crammed with beautiful objects – porcelain vases, sculptures, and orchids – that tie everything together in an opulent, harmonious whole.

The Stranger drops the keys on a console table, pausing to check his reflection in the mirror above, before moving to a cabinet farther in the room. "Whiskey?"

Moth hesitates in the antechamber, uncertain. Then he decides, *the hell with it.* "On the rocks."

The Stranger selects two glasses from the cabinet. He goes into the adjoining kitchen for ice, returns shortly, and reaches for a crystal decanter.

Feeling bolder, Moth steps in, scrutinizing the room. Not unfamiliar with art, among the collection he recognizes a painting by deChirico, a sculpture by Dalí, and a sketch by Picasso. Most likely originals, if the luxury of his surroundings was anything to go by. "Whose apartment is this?"

The Stranger smiles. He pours. "Sit."

Reluctantly, Moth sits on a ridiculously comfortable sofa, despite its appearance to the contrary. The Stranger hands him a heavy tumbler before sitting down across from him. Moth takes a sip, feeling the fire of fine whiskey creep down his throat.

He takes a stab in the dark. "Your name is Cristiano, isn't it?"

"It was. Once."

"And what did you mean, you're surprised to see me alive?"

Cristiano lifts his glass, downing half its contents in one gulp. "You ask a lot of questions. That's the third since you got here." He tucks his hair behind his ear, studying Moth. "Why do you ask so many?"

Defensive, Moth hides behind glibness. "Maybe I'm just curious by nature."

Cristiano tilts his head, long hair slipping over his shoulder like black eels. "I'll tell you why," he says. "You're afraid that people will think you're uninteresting, so you try to distract them from seeing the real you by knocking them off guard with questions carefully selected to make you seem clever, intelligent, and relevant, when in reality they're just used to mask your own insecurities."

Moth's hand, frozen in mid-air, now lowers his tumbler as he stares across the thick glass coffee table at the Stranger. "You're a dick."

"Did you think I was a nice boy?"

"I'm no longer sure that 'boy' is an appropriate term for what you are."

"Touché." Cristiano tilts his glass at Moth, an echo of Moth's gesture earlier at the club. Then his expression shifts, and to Moth he just seems tired. "Well," Cristiano says. "I suppose if it's answers you want..." He trails off, waving his hand in a flourish. "Quite simply, we aren't really human anymore."

In a fucked up way, that made perfect sense. "Then... what are we?"

"There are a number of theories. I do have my favorite, of course. Did you see how they all looked at you at the club, like a god?"

"You think we're gods?"

Cristiano smiles thinly. "Why not?"

"You're fucking vain."

"Devils, then, if that's what you prefer. Or aliens. Or monsters. Other."

Moth knows that he is not an alien. Nor a devil. "Sounds to me like you don't really know what we are."

Cristiano finishes his drink and rises from his chair to fetch the decanter. He replenishes both their glasses before he picks up the thread of the conversation as if there had been no pause. "I know more than you."

"Then tell me."

Cristiano purses his lips in thought. Then he asks, "What's the worst thing that's ever happened to you?"

Moth thinks, *Other than this?* But he doesn't speak it aloud. "What does that have to do with anything?"

"Just humor me. Some terrible memory. Surely you have one."

Moth feels like the other man – or god, or devil, or whatever he is – is mocking him. He doesn't like it. And yet a memory rises up to the surface of his brain, making itself so entirely present that it's as if he is watching a recording of the event, and he can't look away.

He remembers the time he sort of disappeared from home, gone off on a spontaneous bender with some junkies he'd met in Chinatown. For three days, his sole purpose in life was scoring and shooting up more heroin. In-between these two activities, he'd wasted time smoking and nodding off, trading drug stories and drinking lukewarm beers in some stranger's apartment in a bad part of Roxbury. At some point, there'd been a rowdy party, which ended with blowjobs exchanged in a closet, with Moth too high to consider, much less care about, the consequences. The consequences came later, once Moth had come up for air, not sober, exactly, but somewhat self-aware. He called Quentin, apologetic, but it was far too late for an apology to relieve the damage. Quentin, who'd been worried sick, thought Moth lay dead in a ditch of an overdose. Quentin, his voice a tight whisper down the wire, asked what Moth had done, and who he was with? Moth hemmed, but gave him a name, but the unfamiliar male name of Moth's junky friend did nothing to alleviate Quentin's distress. *Did you fuck that guy?* A shrill edge crept into Quentin's normally deep voice. *Quentin, don't ask me that*, Moth said, a non-answer that was really his answer. Quentin's emotional meltdown followed in the form of angry words and accusations. Moth could only fumble with the most perfunctory of responses, a defense mechanism having clicked on and caused him to shrink back within himself in the ugly face of that confrontation. At the end of Quentin's melodramtic rant, he said, quite quietly, *You've killed me*, and then the line went dead.

When Quentin hung up, guilt and love and hate gnawed through the edges of Moth's dissolving high, guilt because he'd fucked up, hate for Quentin for making him feel the guilt. He tried calling back, again and again, raging at the ring tone until finally, after what seemed an eternity, someone picked up. It was Will, their neighbor and Quentin's friend, also distraught, telling Moth that Quentin was in an ambulance on his way to the hospital because he'd put his fist through a window, cutting himself badly. Shouting at Moth, Will demanded, *Mike, what did you* do? With Moth, guilt-ridden and helpless on the other end of the line in Roxbury, thinking, *Oh, god, what have I done?*

Cristiano watches him. "So. Thought of something, did you?" he asks. "And how do you feel about it now?"

Moth considers how he feels, which is now at a distance from the memory. As if he had seen it in a movie a long time ago, or like it had happened to someone else. He shrugs.

"That's what's happening to you. You're a heartless monster." He smiles that thin smile again, bemused. "Isn't it wonderful?"

Moth considers the implications of losing his ability to feel, to empathize. If this is the case, it won't be long before he is bereft of all traces of humanity, which will mean he *is*, on some level, a monster.

Or at least a sociopath.

"That doesn't explain anything," Moth points out. "The... mechanism of it."

"Fine." Cristiano swirls his tumbler. "You know those frogs that secrete toxins through their skin, toxins that the natives use to tip their arrows in? We're like those frogs, except that, for us, the toxin will continue to build up in our system and, at a certain point, in about four or five days, need to be expelled."

"Expelled," Moth repeats slowly.

"To put it in terms I think you'll understand, you're basically a walking syringe full of heroin, and when you have sex, it ends when you inject them."

Moth fidgets, thinking of the bone needle. "Injecting them with this 'toxin' means they become like us?"

"Oh, no. Not usually. Most of the time, they don't survive. If I may give you some advice, I'd suggest you pick your victims carefully: women, the young, the sickly. Drug addicts."

Cristiano's words sink in slowly, like bodies in a river weighted with bricks. Anger spikes Moth's blood, and curls one hand hard around his glass, the other into a fist. The nerve of this man, coming into Moth's life, as if Moth's life were Tokyo and he were Godzilla, trampling everything and leaving nothing except destruction. In his mouth, Moth's tongue is thick. "That's murder," he finally manages to say.

Expressionless, Cristiano fingers his glass. "It's them or us," he says, eyes glimmering like ancient coins in the dim light. "So you're going to have to make a choice."

~

Across Urbino, within his cocoon, Arturo dreams.

He is a child, bedridden by fever and pain. His joints burn, his bones ache, the sheets scratch his overly sensitive and sticky skin. His mother, face creased with worry, leans down to press her lips to his forehead. He recoils from the touch, squirming. She smells like lilacs, the scent from a French milled soap.

His limbs are heavy, his head light. Within the balloon casing of his head, his thoughts are muddled. He floats through the day, untethered and unfocused, drifting in and out of sleep until a knife of pain in his belly awakens him.

He cries out, his mother comes. Arturo cannot be soothed, he sobs and cannot stop. He hears his parents' voices in the hall, angry with panic, and then his father is bundling him up, carrying him down to the car—

—hits a slick of ice. The front tires swerve dangerously to the right. Panicked, Arturo instinctively jerks the wheel to the left, foot slamming down on the useless brakes. Spinning, the Fiat shoots over the icy road, completely out of his control. He grinds his foot down into the brake pedal as his hands try to compensate at the wheel, but it is too late. It all happens in a second. Through the windshield, small snowflakes, reflecting the headlights, swirl through the darkness, followed by a quick flash of steel. The car's front-end slams up against the guardrail, sudden and hard, twisting plastic and crumpling metal, the safety belt compulsively catching at the moment of impact, bruising the skin above his sternum and he—

—is sitting on a bench in the park with Stefano. Spring sunlight splashes down on their open newspapers, and then Stefano says, *Check out that girl*. Arturo glances up, and when he sees her, his heart quickens. He is convinced that this is love at first sight, that this young woman with the dark hair and glasses is his destiny. Without saying a word, he folds up his newspaper, rises from the bench and follows her out of the park, onto the streets heavy with fading light.

In the dark corner, the cocoon is still. Within, the man who was Arturo dreams his butterfly dreams. He does not dream like mortals, to remember. He dreams to forget. He becomes forgetful and he becomes.

FOURTEEN

Moth runs into Sam in the square. Sam, alone and bored, suggests they go back to his place to drink some vodka. This invitation is only extended after he tells Moth an abbreviated version of the Lisa story. How the ambulance came and whisked her away to the hospital, where the doctor injected her with Narcan, thus saving her life, and how nobody bothered to report it to the police. All's well that ends well, except, Sam reveals, Orazio is still pissed off at him about what happened.

Moth vaguely wonders if Orazio is pissed off because Sam almost killed someone or because Sam dipped into Orazio's stash in order to impress a girl. Probably both.

He also wonders if Sam would be safe alone with him. He still has one or two days to go before the toxin will reach a critical point in his body, and he'll need to have sex with someone. One thing Cristiano emphasized before Moth left was that there had to be actual penetration of a living thing, thus ruling masturbation out. So, even if he were to seduce Sam tonight, at least from what information he'd gathered from Cristiano, the lesser amount of toxin he'd release probably wouldn't kill Sam.

Probably.

Strangely, he finds that he has fewer qualms about killing Sam than he thought he would.

However, as Sam peers expectantly into his face, Moth doesn't note any particular desire in the younger man's face beyond the need for companionship and alcohol. So he agrees to go.

As Sam unlocks the door and lets Moth into the apartment, Moth thinks about the irony of his situation. Now he can have anyone he wants, but the men he wants – healthy, attractive men in their prime – are now off-limits, unless he wants to risk making more monsters, which, Cristiano pointed out, with a heavy sense of self-preservation, would invariably lead to a gold-eyed monster hunt, and the downfall of all of them as a species.

"Orazio?" Moth asks as he drops his jacket on the mattress next to him.

"He's gone out," Sam replies vaguely from the doorway.

Moth listens to the sounds of clinking in the kitchen. A moment later, Sam reappears with two drinking glasses, each a third filled with vodka, as well as the bottle, which he puts on the floor between them. Moth picks up the bottle, admiring the label which he can't read, but which is decorated with black and red birds drawn in an abstract manner.

"It's real Russian vodka," Sam reveals. "Someone gave it to Orazio as a gift."

Moth sets down the bottle. "Are you sure he won't mind that we're drinking it?"

Sam shrugs.

"How passive aggressive of you," Moth teases, but takes a sip of the vodka. He doesn't care much for the taste of it, but he drinks it anyway.

Sam ignores the taunt. "Are you holding?"

Moth shakes his head.

Sam tries but cannot quite keep the disappointment from his face. "I don't know where Orazio hid the stash. Assuming there *is* a stash."

"Ah," Moth says. Given how little the boys own and how small the apartment is, he doubts that it's even possible to have an unfindable hiding place. "Orazio is that pissed off, is he?"

Sam gives him a sidelong glance. "You really haven't seen him since that night?"

Moth shakes his head again.

"Oh." Sam makes a strange little grimace.

"What?" Moth demands. "What was *that* face?"

"Nothing," Sam says quickly. He toys with his glass, speaking haltingly. "It's just, well, my brother... He hasn't had a boyfriend in a really long time."

This gives Moth pause. "You think I'm Orazio's boyfriend?"

"Well..." Sam says, *I saw you* implicit in his expression. "Aren't you?"

It suddenly strikes Moth that Sam's look is now somewhat hopeful.

"No, I'm not," he says, and watches that flicker of hope start to die. "I mean, we're very good friends."

"But you guys like each other, right? I mean... I probably shouldn't be telling you this, but you're like the first guy Orazio's been with, in a non-exploitative way, in, like, two years. So, you could, you know, go out."

Moth eyes him with suspicion. "Did Orazio say something about me?"

"Nooo," Sam says. "I mean, since Juan's party, he started referring to you as 'that fucking American boy'."

Moth snorts softly. "Apparently, passive-aggressiveness runs in your family."

Sam's mouth tightens. "Well? Are you dating my brother or not?"

"It's not that simple," Moth says gently. But it strikes him, at this moment, that having a boyfriend is no longer a possibility for him. He's now a flesh-and-blood machine only capable of killing everyone he loves. It also explains why Cristiano, right before Moth left, had proposed they form a partnership. At least this way, Cristiano would no longer have to be alone.

"Okay," Sam relents. "But I warn you – if you hurt my brother, I'll hurt you."

Moth nearly chokes on his drink. *"You* will hurt *me?* And may I ask how you'd propose to do that?"

Sam smiles slyly. "I'd ask Juan to kick your ass."

Moth laughs. "Fair enough," he says.

FIFTEEN

Saturday falls down around him, darkness bleeding the color out of the sky, and drowning the hills of Urbino in shadow. The stars, shining brightly, crowd around him, and a harvest moon seems to hang just above his head, almost close enough to touch.

Using Arturo's keys, he lets himself into the apartment. He flips on a few lights. He checks on the cocoon before making himself a small pot of espresso in the kitchen. Once the espresso is ready, he takes a cup, along with the ashtray, into the bedroom.

He sits on the bed. Drinks the espresso. He smokes as he waits for Arturo to emerge. He thinks. He thinks about how he finally managed to wrangle the story out of Sam about what had happened between Dominik and Orazio. Sam was vague, didn't know all the details, but it involved Dominik's boyfriend at the time and some heroin. The boyfriend had approached Orazio, looking to buy. Orazio, always on the lookout for an opportunity to rip other people off, had cut the heroin so thoroughly that Dominik and his boyfriend ended up snorting almost pure baby formula. When later confronted by the boyfriend, Orazio talked with his fists, leaving the boy with a black eye, some bruises, and an understandable thirst for revenge.

Moth thinks about Dominik, how prettily the boy smiled at him earlier this afternoon at Basili's, offering him a coffee and a *panino* on the house, which Moth accepted, asking Moth if he planned on going to The Dive tonight. When Moth answered in a non-committal, vaguely affirmative kind of way, Dominik smiled and said maybe they'd see each other there.

He thinks about how he can feel the threads of the alien fabric unfurling in his veins and scratching up against his organs, driving him to feed its increasing and relentless need.

When he's tired of thinking, he takes out his little book of poems and writes, tracing the memory of Orazio's naked vulnerability across the page. Writing stream-of-consciousness about Orazio, there is a kindness and a certain sentimentality to his words, which surprises him.

He has just stubbed out his third cigarette when the cocoon cracks open and Arturo worms his way out. Arturo, dazed and incoherent, does not struggle against the hands which pull him onto the bed, wrapping the comforter around his shoulders, nor does he refuse the glass of water thrust into his hands, as a faraway voice commands him: *Drink this. You're dehydrated. It will help.*

He drinks the water. Comes to his senses. He remembers who he is as he recognizes where he is and the person now sitting, at some distance, on the bed across from him. He remembers what happened to him. He also remembers his anger, but now he is too weak to fight.

Moth peers into his face. Gold eyes stare blankly back at him. "Are you okay, Arturo?"

He feels only the barest flicker of rage. "Why?" he asks, voice weary. "Why did you do this to me?"

Moth's mouth tightens. "I didn't know. I didn't know what would happen."

Arturo sighs. "Why are you even here? To gloat?"

"No. But I have answers."

Arturo sets the glass down on the nightstand, pulling the comforter tighter around himself before he leans back against the headboard. "Fine," he says grudgingly. "Give them to me."

As Moth talks, Arturo closes his eyes and listens. His entire being is focused on the words like spiders spinning out of Moth's mouth. He listens as Moth talks about meeting the Stranger and what the Stranger told him. Finally, at a certain point, he can't listen anymore. He opens his eyes, says, "Enough."

Moth falls silent.

On the nightstand, a clock ticks.

Finally, Arturo asks, "What if it's a virus?"

"If it's a virus, it's like no virus I've ever heard of," Moth says. "What if it is?"

"If it's a virus, maybe someone could find a cure."

Moth wonders how to say *grasping at straws* in Italian. He doesn't know. Instead he says, "If it is a virus, then it's probably too late for a cure for us. Three days of transformation in a cocoon? For all we know, even our internal organs have changed. And it's not like we can just waltz off to the doctor for x-rays."

Arturo laughs, a weak bark tinged with bitterness. "You're such an asshole."

"Look on the bright side. Now you can have any woman you want."

"*Cass,*" Arturo mutters. "I like women. What kind of person do you think I am? You think I could just murder someone in cold blood?"

"You will, if you want to survive and not make more of us."

"And that Cristiano guy told you this? How do you know he wasn't lying?"

"I'd say he was telling the truth, considering the evidence,.."

"Wait," Arturo says, as something previously mentioned suddenly clicks. "What day's today?"

"Saturday."

"Damn it, Chiara will be home tomorrow."

He hadn't meant to speak that thought aloud and is surprised when Moth answers. "Well, *that* should be interesting."

Arturo considers the situation. If what Moth said is true, then Chiara would arrive home at the same time his need would be hitting its peak. Arturo always wanted to protect Chiara, but he'd never imagined the thing he'd have to protect her from would be himself.

And there is one person he can blame. He lifts his weary head, and snarls at Moth. "In case I didn't make it clear the other night – I never want to see you again. I don't want to talk to you. Fuck! I don't want to have anything to do with you. Just go fuck yourself."

Moth stands. He reaches into his pocket and pulls out a small case, which he sets on the nightstand next to Arturo, along with Arturo's keys. "Contacts," he explains. "Green ones. They probably won't fit you right, so they won't be very comfortable, but it beats trying to explain to people why your eye color suddenly changed."

Arturo watches Moth leave. Huddles inside his blanket. Shudders involuntarily when he hears the door slam. Fingers the contact lens case, then notices that there's something on the floor.

It is Moth's little notebook.

~

Within the larger cycle of big cities and small towns, the cycle of falling in love and relationships falling apart, the cycle of heady heroin binges and ugly withdrawals, there are smaller cycles of daily living. Patterns of behavior that become ingrained as habits, and because it is already habit, Moth finds himself halfway between Arturo's apartment and The Dive before he even questions where he's going.

Habit also propels him to check his wrist for the missing watch, even though he knows that it is already somewhere after eleven o'clock and not too early to go to The Dive. He considers his options, which are few. Vaguely he's already decided that the best course of action is to find a lone leech at the club, preferably one from out of town, preferably one who's not unbearably unattractive, and to whisk him away to somewhere dark and quiet, where they won't be seen.

Moth rubs at his wrist bones, thinking about how he could probably use his influence on Orazio in order to convince him to return the Movado, assuming that Orazio hasn't already sold it in order to buy junk, and, since he's already going to The Dive to find a victim, he might as well look for Orazio, too. Kill two junkies with one stone. One figuratively, of course.

In the club he spies Juan, sitting with Sergio and Valentino, half-empty glasses and overflowing ashtrays crowding the small table between them. Moth greets them all with customary kisses then asks if they've seen Orazio.

White teeth flash like lighthouse signals in the Spaniard's face. "I suggest you check the bathroom," Juan says. To Moth, it sounds more like an order than a suggestion. "But do be polite and knock first."

"Thanks," Moth says. "I'll be back."

Juan tips an imaginary hat at him.

Before he goes, Moth can't help but notice how all the men regard him hungrily and hide it with varying degrees of success. Perhaps Sergio, due to his age and inexperience, is the most obvious. As the luscious Sicilian boy undresses him with his eyes, Moth feels the pang of regret born from lost opportunity.

In that moment it strikes him that the transformation isn't viral. Or alien. Or divine. In that moment, it's a curse.

He slips through the still-thin crowd then down a narrow flight of stairs, his boot heels echoing loudly on the concrete steps. Other than two boys smoking and jostling by the mirror to fix their hair, Moth doesn't see anyone. He pauses, watching the boys preen for another minute before they bounce back up the stairs.

He vaguely wonders if he missed Orazio, or if the young man is hustling or doing something else not so legal in Rats' Alley. But in a moment of inspiration, Moth crouches down to peek under the stall doors.

Not only does he spy feet – one pair clad in boots, the other in shiny patent leather loafers – but there is also a pair of knees on the ground.

Moth considers slipping out quietly. Then he thinks *fuck it.* He raps lightly on the stall door. "Orazio?"

A pause, and then the door to the stall swings open. Orazio leans against one of the walls, receiving a blowjob from the man kneeling at his feet. Orazio's lips curl up in a charming smile, fringed with secrets. He seems genuinely pleased to see Moth. "Where have you been?"

Moth tries not to stare brazenly down at Orazio's leech *du jour*, catching only a glimpse of shoulder-length auburn hair over a dark jacket. He takes out a pack of Marlboros and taps one loose. "Around."

"Around," Orazio repeats, sounding amused. He snags the cigarette from between Moth's lips, putting it between his own. "Michele, you're a devil of a fellow."

Moth smiles, lighting the cigarette for Orazio. "I know."

The auburn-haired man draws back. Still on his knees, he looks up at Moth. In English he asks Orazio, "Friend of yours?"

Orazio lazily packs his half-mast erection back into his jeans and responds in English. "Yes. A very good friend."

The john pushes a lock of bright hair out of his eyes, assessing Moth, then lets his hands fall to his thighs as he leans back on his heels for a better look. His eyes are bright blue, his skin pale, his accent well-bred British. "Do you think your friend would be willing to join us?"

Moth and Orazio exchange a glance.

"I'd make it worth your while," he says.

Orazio steps out of the stall to pull Moth aside. "Well? What do you think?" When Moth doesn't answer right away, Orazio adds, "He's an easy mark. We'll split the money fifty-fifty. This guy's rich. Did you see his shoes? Ferragamo's."

Not for the first time, Moth wonders about Orazio's relationship with fashion. Sure, he was aware that Orazio has Armani in his closet, but he still couldn't quite grasp the concept of a well-dressed junky hustler. Certainly the American junkies he'd known didn't dress half so well. He thinks that he would like to ask Juan if Spanish junkies are equally fashionable, or if it is a strictly Italian phenomenon.

"Well?" Orazio prompts.

Moth thinks about how it's always been a point of pride that he's never taken money for sex. He thinks about how predictably despicable Orazio is, already plotting to rip off his customer. It's not that he would ever admit to feeling morally superior to Orazio, but some small part of him does. So the old Moth never would have agreed to it.

The new Moth, however, recalls how delectably Orazio writhed beneath him, begging to be taken, and how it had felt to possess that sort of power. He has also judged the john as being a perfect victim: a man past his prime, alone in a foreign country, one willing to pay for sexual services, so why not dabble in drugs? Which is precisely what the authorities would think upon finding the foreigner's body, full of toxin.

Of course, given the choice between the sultry young hustler and the middle-aged john, Moth would much rather fuck Orazio. Unfortunately, that would most likely kill him. A scenario which Moth would like to avoid, even though the idea of it, like the idea of killing Sam, bothers him less than he thought it would.

As Orazio says, he's a devil of a fellow.

"Fuck it," Moth says. "I'm in."

~

In the hotel lobby, Moth is only half-listening to Orazio's exchange with the clerk at the front desk, who inquires whether they'll be staying the night because, if so, he will need their IDs, either a passport or a *carta d'identità*, but Orazio smooth talks, saying they're just going up for a quick drink with their uncle.

Moth wonders if the hotel clerk knows what's really going on. For that matter, he wonders if the guy knows Orazio. It is a small town, after all.

The john steps up to the counter. "Is there a problem?"

"No, sir." The clerk slides the room key across the counter. "Have a pleasant night."

The hotel is inside the city walls, so for that reason alone, Moth assumes that it must be expensive. It's also in an old building, which means that the lobby is small. However, with its subdued lighting and tasteful Old World décor, it's quite cozy. The place is so authentically old and Old World, in fact, that there is no elevator, so they head up three flights of stairs to what the Italians, unlike Americans, call the second floor.

"It's a bit of a walk, but worth it for the view," the john assures them as he ushers them inside the room.

Like the lobby, the room is small but elegant. Once inside, Orazio throws himself down on the matrimonial bed, bouncing on it as if to ascertain its integrity for the festivities to come. Moth, on the other hand, crosses to the curtained window. The john moves to the mini-bar. "Drink?"

Orazio stops bouncing, and answers for both of them. "Yes, please."

With elegant hands and long fingers, the john unwraps clean glasses, and twists caps off tiny bottles of liquor. "You boys both from Urbino?"

Orazio smiles. "My friend is from Urbino. I am from Potenza, in the South."

Moth pulls back the heavy drapes to look out. Across from him, the Palazzo Ducale dominates the city in all its Renaissance glory, one of its turrets nearly piercing the moon. He tosses a glance at Orazio. "You really should check out this view."

Orazio shrugs, the picture of indifference, but rises to join Moth at the window. He flicks a glance through the window pane, then says, "Shit built by dead people."

"That describes most of Italy," Moth says. He gazes at history once more before turning his attention back to Orazio. "You never told me where you're from."

"I came to Urbino for school."

Moth knew little about the South, other than it was poorer than the North. Picturesque, but rustic. "What's Potenza like?"

Orazio shrugs again. "It's home," he says. Then adds, "Not a lot of tourists. You wouldn't like it."

"You live anywhere else?" Moth expects him to say no, as Italians tend to not change their residences frequently, but Orazio launches into a story about a brief stay in Naples, where he ran guns for the *Camorra*, the local mafia. Before the story ends, however, the john approaches them.

"Such a beautiful language you speak," he says as he hands each of them a drink. "It's like music."

Moth and Orazio sip their drinks. Vodka tonics fizzle like sunshine on their tongues.

"Oh," Orazio says in Italian, as an afterthought to Moth. "He's looking for an Italian 'experience.' So don't let him know you're American." As an afterthought to the afterthought, he adds, "In fact, it's better if you don't speak any English at all."

What Moth knows about hustling would fit in a thimble, but as a poet there is one thing he knows well, and that is human nature and the thirst for new experiences. Besides, he figures it's just easier to go along with it. "*Va beh.*"

Orazio turns to the Englishman, smiling that smile that transforms his face from sullenness to boyish charm. "What do you like?" The john leans forward, his finger following a wave in Orazio's hair to subsequently trace the line of Orazio's jaw. Orazio's expression softens. Moth knows that it is just an act, but admires the skill of his friend's artifice.

"I like to watch," he says.

Orazio's smile becomes more knowing. "Just watch?"

"For now."

Orazio turns to Moth. He places his free hand on Moth's shoulder. Through his leather jacket, Moth feels the pressure of Orazio's fingers. "Let's give him a show, shall we?"

This wasn't exactly what Moth had planned. But he doesn't stop Orazio when he leans forward, mouth seeking mouth. For a moment they kiss, and in that moment, Moth feels the need inside him suddenly expand, consuming all his other thoughts. As they kiss, Orazio's hips strain against him, his erection immediate and crushed against Moth's hip. When they part, Orazio is breathless, eyes glazed over, his pupils pinned.

Moth is aware of the john watching them with interest, but he doesn't care. All he cares about is getting inside Orazio, getting some sort of release. In a few steps, Moth has set their drinks aside and maneuvered Orazio to the bed below him.

Orazio opens his arms.

Moth lingers above him, drinking in the sight. Face smeared with desire, Orazio is beautiful.

Moth thinks about how it takes a long time to create something beautiful but only a moment to destroy. He wants to destroy Orazio. Orazio is his only friend in the world. He can only rely on himself. This is murder. He's a killer now. He's a man. He's a monster. Should he? Or shouldn't he? Orazio is his only friend in the world.

The dark thing wants.

Orazio waits.

SIXTEEN

Arturo chooses his clothing carefully before he goes to pick up Chiara at the bus station. He puts on his fine corduroy pants and a subtly striped brown and green knit top, both Armani. Sunglasses, a clean shave, and pointy-toed dress shoes complete the look. He's not so much dressing to impress as he is dressing to maintain distance. Like Moth's long, dye-streaked hair, torn jeans, and tattoo, Arturo's look transmits an implicit message of *I've got everything together*. It is armor.

Also, Arturo needs to believe that he hasn't been turned into an involuntary killer. He needs to believe in free will, that he can master whatever is happening to him. After all, monsters don't wear Armani.

The bus is late, Arturo waits nearly half an hour in the parking lot outside of Porta Valbona when he finally lays eyes on Chiara. She waves, he approaches, they kiss hello, then Arturo carries her suitcase to the car.

At the car, Chiara whistles loudly as her gaze sweeps over him. "Are you dressed up for a reason?"

He unlocks her door before moving around the car to unlock his own. "I just felt like it."

She smiles. "Boy. Your other girlfriend sure is lucky."

Arturo plays along. "She's eternally grateful."

As he drives them home, she tells him about the conference, and her own presentation which involved an awkward mishap with the microphone, but Arturo scarcely listens. Instead, he's distracted by his thoughts, most of which revolve around his growing need to have sex with her. It's an unbearable itch in his libido, just being in the car with her, one he desperately needs to scratch.

She trails off. Arturo feels her gaze as hot feelers on his skin. "What?" he asks.

"Nothing," she says softly. "I was just thinking about how handsome you are."

Arturo smiles thinly and pretends to focus on the road.

At home, he carries her suitcase up the stairs and into the bedroom. He drops the suitcase on the bed, and then turns to find her standing behind him, having followed him into the bedroom without his realizing it.

Chiara steps forward, pushes his sunglasses up onto his head, and kisses him. A real kiss, both soft and exigent. He feels his own need flare up again. The itch increases exponentially until it becomes genuinely painful, like all his organs are made of sandpaper, rubbing frantically against each other in his abdominal cavity.

Only a small part of him, the part that loves her, does not want to be alone in the bedroom with her, does not want to be kissing her, does not want to risk harming her. To this part of himself Arturo clings, forcing himself to pull away. The movement is abrupt enough to seem calculated. He takes a step back, readjusting the sunglasses on his face.

Chiara, her expression half-dreamy, half disappointed, blinks in confusion. She rubs at her mouth with the back of her hand. "You taste bitter," she says.

"Must be the coffee I drank."

Chiara frowns a little. "You don't taste like coffee," she says. "You taste... medicinal." The frown fades, then transforms into a coy smile. "Why don't you brush your teeth and then come back to the bedroom?"

There is nothing that the dark thing in Arturo wants more. It longs to take and destroy, to crush her with its power, to fill her with its intoxicating poison.

Clinging to that shred of love, Arturo pushes past her. "I have to go to work."

The words come out cold and harsh. Chiara's smile vanishes in an instant. "Arturo – what's wrong? Is it something I said?"

"Nothing's wrong."

Chiara follows him into the living room, watches him scoop up his keys from the counter. "I don't believe you," she says. "Something's wrong. Was it because I said you tasted funny? Was it something else I said? Why won't you talk to me?"

Arturo needs to get away from her before something terrible happens. He knows it. He has a stray thought, nonsensical: *Why can't she understand?* But she has no idea what has happened to him and can't understand. And he can't tell her.

He growls in exasperation. "I said I have to go!"

Chiara flinches, then becomes perfectly still. In all their time together, Arturo has never raised his voice with her before. She presses her lips together in order to seal the words in her mouth from escaping, and to keep her lips from quivering. Confused, hurt, she doesn't know what to do. Speechless, she watches Arturo storm out of the apartment, slamming the door behind him, before her first tears fall.

Moth wakes up on Juan's sofa with a crick in his neck and a bad taste in his mouth. The latter most likely due to the malt liquor he drank last night with Juan and the boys, still at the same dirty table right where he'd left them, when he'd eventually returned to The Dive.

He sits up, rubbing his neck, and considers how he feels. He doesn't feel good. It takes an effort to get to his feet and make his way to the bathroom. As he passes Juan's bedroom, he notices that the door is open and the unmade bed is empty. Further exploration reveals that he's alone in the apartment, and that Juan has left him a note on the kitchen stove.

Ciao bello, Moth reads. *I had to go to work, but I didn't want to wake you. You're so cute when you're sleeping. Make yourself some coffee. Un bacio, J.*

Moth checks the moka on the stove, then turns on the gas when he determines that it's already been prepared. While he waits for the espresso, he smokes a cigarette, flicking the ashes into the drain of the sink. The cigarette doesn't help him feel any better. He feels rattled, and thin as a paper doll. Junk sick.

The coffee does calm his nerves somewhat, but does nothing good for his stomach. He eats a slice of Juan's bread, thinking about how Juan flirted with him last night in the car while Valentino drove them home. A flirtation which Moth ended as soon as they walked in the door, when Moth most definitively stated that he was exhausted and just wanted to sleep. Juan, in gentlemanly fashion, retreated to his own room for the night after fetching him a pillow and blanket.

He also thinks about how different his night would have been if he'd returned to The Dive only five minutes sooner, since then he would have crossed paths with Dominik. This according to Juan, who added, with a knowing smirk, that Dominik had come specifically looking for Moth.

It's only when he's put on his boots that he realizes that he doesn't have a ride from Juan's apartment – far outside the city walls – and he has no one to call.

Resigned, he starts walking, out of the complex and down the winding road towards the medieval town. He puts his thumb out to passing cars. Luckily, the third car stops, and a business man drops him off at Porta Valbona.

Moth is completely unaware that, just two hours ago, Arturo was standing in the same parking lot, waiting for Chiara.

Moth climbs up a hill to the center of town. After a cursory sweep of the square, he climbs up another hill. Stops part way up at Orazio's building. After being buzzed in, he climbs the stairs to find Sam waiting at the door. "Hey."

"Hey."

Moth steps in. "Orazio?"

"He should be back soon," Sam reveals. He fidgets uncontrollably. "*Farfalla?* Are you, uh, sure you *want* to see my brother? He's totally pissed off at you right now."

"Ah. I kind of figured as much."

Sam eyes him curiously. "Look. It's really none of my business, but... well, he said that the two of you had gone to some guy's hotel room."

"Yeah. And?"

Sam blinks. In that moment, his perception of who Moth is irrevocably changes. Moth can almost feel Sam's regard for him drop by several degrees.

"And that's all he said," Sam reveals. "Though he started referring to you as 'that fucking American boy' again, only not in a good way."

Moth knows that Sam wants information. Maybe Sam even wants him to defend himself or justify his actions. On top of that, he's not surprised that Orazio is pissed off at him. Things between them had just started getting interesting when Moth, seized by guilt, became unable to go through with it. Tearing himself away from Orazio, he had practically bolted from the room.

"I think I lost him some money."

"I see," Sam says, looking somewhat relieved.

Moth straightens his back, not quite looking at Sam. "I'm not here to see your brother."

"Oh?"

"I just came to pick up my stuff."

"Oh, yeah? Are you going somewhere?"

Moth still can't quite meet Sam's eyes. "Yeah. I'm leaving town."

"Woah. Really? That's... sudden."

Somewhere between the leech's hotel room and The Dive, Moth began entertaining the notion of leaving, maybe of even accepting Cristiano's offer of working as a team, although he is less certain that this is his best option. Then, while waiting for the espresso to brew in Juan's kitchen, he thought about how Urbino was too small to compete for victims with Arturo, and how, in a certain sense, that made them enemies. Arturo had certainly treated him like one. What had existed between them had existed mostly in Moth's head, and even that was now over.

"I'll just get my things," Moth says and ducks quickly out of the room before Sam can say anything.

In Orazio's bedroom, it takes him little time to pack up his meager belongings. He finds the Movado in the table drawer next to the condoms. Obviously Orazio hadn't sold it, after all.

Moth has just finished slipping the watch into his bag when he hears the front door open, then shut.

He hears Sam's voice. "*Farfalla*'s here."

Orazio mutters something too quiet to hear, then, "What's he doing here?"

"Came to get his stuff. Said he's leaving town."

Moth steps out. He sees Orazio, arms crossed, standing in the middle of the room, a sour look on his face. Oozing hostility, he stabs Moth with his eyes. "You're leaving town?"

"That was the idea, yeah."

Orazio wraps his arms tighter around himself, rocking back on his heels, then forward. "You going back to America?"

Moth adjusts the bag over his shoulder. If meeting Sam's eyes was difficult, meeting Orazio's is impossible. "I haven't decided where I'm going yet."

Orazio eyes Moth's bag. "And you were just going to take off without saying anything to me."

It's more a statement of the obvious than a question, but there, in Orazio's statement, is an undercurrent of real emotion. The thought suddenly strikes Moth, clear as spring water: *Orazio loves me.*

"I didn't think you'd want to see me after last night," Moth mumbles.

Orazio pauses. He's about to say something, then shoots a glance at Sam. Something in his expression shifts, softening. "Yeah. Well. I should have known better. There's a rule about not bringing an amateur to a threesome."

"Jesus," Sam mutters. He stands up, reaching for his jacket. "That's *way* more information than I needed to hear."

Orazio grabs him by the shoulder, stopping his trajectory. "Where are you going?"

"I'm pretending to go buy some cigarettes." Sam shrugs off Orazio's hand. He stops before Moth. "If I don't see you again, have a nice life."

Moth thanks him and the door clicks shut. Orazio narrows his eyes at Moth, hostile again. "That was really a douche move you pulled last night, you fucker."

Orazio loves me. Moth watches Orazio take out his cigarettes and light one. He doesn't offer one to Moth.

"Sorry. I just couldn't go through with it. Not with that guy watching."

Orazio takes a long drag. He's thinking that this is the second time that he'd started having sex with Moth without actually having sex. Given last night, he's now questioning if Moth would have really gone through with it in the first place, or if Moth was just playing with him. "You didn't seem to care when everybody watched Dominik blow you."

Shit. Jealousy rears its head. Moth has an inkling about why Orazio shot Dominik up with the speedball: an unconscious – or maybe even conscious – desire to kill him. Moth scrambles for the right thing to say. "That's different," Moth says. "That guy last night was old and creepy."

"Yeah, whatever," Orazio mumbles. Then something cold and calculated comes into his blue as Spring skies eyes. "Well, no one is watching now. You want to finish what we started before you go?"

This is the other reason why Moth has decided to leave town. He doesn't really want to kill his friends. Even resisting Juan, to whom Moth had never felt any attraction, had been difficult. Being alone with Orazio and his need now was downright *dangerous.*

He has no other choice. In order to save them both, he has to shut Orazio down. "I don't think it's a good idea."

To his credit, Orazio's expression doesn't change. He shrugs, moving to flick his cigarette over the ashtray. Then his eyes, frost cold, slowly sweep up and down Moth. "You're not taking off with my shirt, you prick. Give it back, and then you can fuck off."

Moth drops his bag, then his jacket. He peels off Orazio's shirt and tosses it down at the younger man's feet. Shoves his hand into his bag and digs out what he hopes is his least dirty shirt. As he does this, Orazio watches him venomously, sucking hard on his cigarette.

Moth slams the door behind him. Orazio stares at the door for a long time, thinking about how he'll probably never see Moth again. He thinks about how unexpectedly shitty that feels. "Fucking American boy," he mutters to the empty room.

But to every problem there is a solution. And for Orazio, there is only ever one solution.

He puts out his cigarette, then goes to the bedroom closet where he retrieves his secret stash from a coat pocket. In the bedroom, he takes out his works, lining them up neatly on the table. After he fetches a lemon half from the kitchen, he kneels down before the table, and from the glassine wrap he taps the usual amount of heroin into the black-bottomed spoon.

Reconsidering, he taps some more.

~

At Arturo's apartment door, Moth steels his nerves before knocking.

He'd considered calling first, but decided that he didn't want to give Arturo the option of saying no. Instead, he had trekked all the way beyond the city walls. His plan is simple: knock on the door, demand that Arturo hand over the little notebook he had so foolishly forgotten the last time he was here, and then make his escape. They wouldn't even have to really speak to each other.

Pulling himself together, however, is no easy feat. He still feels ill, his nerves rubbed raw, and every part of him suffers. Since this morning, it's only gotten worse. Vaguely he wonders exactly how much longer he can go on before the toxin building up inside him kills him.

He steps forward and knocks on the door.

Chiara answers.

For some reason it hadn't occurred to him that Arturo's girlfriend would be home, even though Arturo had mentioned it. Surprised, he stares dumbly at her.

"Oh, it's you," she says. "If you're looking for Arturo, he's at the office."

He sees that her eyes are red, and her face is puffy, as if she'd just been crying. "Actually, I don't need to see Arturo. I came to pick up a notebook I left here," he says. Then, "Are you okay?"

Chiara hastily wipes at her face. "Yes, I'm fine. You said you left a notebook? Come in."

Moth shuffles awkwardly inside.

Treading lightly, Chiara drifts towards the kitchen. "Could I offer you something to drink? A coffee?"

"Sure," Moth says, an automatic response to anyone who offers him coffee. Even though he has no idea when Arturo will return and would like to avoid seeing him if possible.

As Chiara sets about making espresso, Moth scans the room. He doesn't see the notebook lying about. He ignores the temptation to go into the bedroom and look for himself. Turning back around, he sees Chiara looking at him, almost expectantly.

He settles on making small talk. He used to be quite good at it, in another life. "So, I heard you were out of town for a conference?"

Chiara opens the cupboard and removes an espresso cup. She sets in the counter, giving Moth a long look. "Can I ask you something about Arturo?"

No. "Of course."

"Did something happen while I was away? Or did he say something to you?"

"Something? What kind of something?"

"I don't know," Chiara says, looking lost. "It's just... when I got home, Arturo was acting strangely. He wouldn't talk to me." On the counter her hands clench into fists. She takes a deep breath, making a concerted effort to unclench them. "Do you know anything at all?"

Moth considers a number of possible responses, none of which involve the truth. "I'm sorry. It's not like Arturo and I are friends, or anything."

"Yes. I suppose you're not." She chews on her bottom lip, thoughtful. "Sorry if I put you on the spot."

"No, it's fine," Moth says. "But... do you want to talk about it?"

Heavy dark hair falls down around her chin as she stares down into the abyss of the empty cup. When she lifts her head again, she is smiling. Forced and fake. "No," she says lightly. "I'm sure it will all work out in the end."

Moth suppresses his disappointment. Then he mentally kicks himself for wanting to know what happened between her and Arturo. He's leaving town in part to get away from Arturo, so why does he care what happens to that prick?

Next to Chiara, the moka gurgles. Moth watches her pour out a cup, then add two small spoonfuls of sugar without asking. Then he recalls that they'd already had coffee once together at Basili's.

"Good memory," he remarks as she brings him the cup.

Chiara's eyes meet his. She lays a hand on his arm. "You're very kind," she says. *And you're a beautiful man.*

Moth's breath catches in his throat. Of course he would have the same effect on Chiara as he had on Orazio, Juan and the john. Of course he'd noticed that he'd been receiving looks from members of both sexes since he'd emerged from the cocoon. Even before that, after Cristiano had fucked him in the alley, there had been hints: Orazio's unexpected arousal, the hungry gazes of both men and women, Dominik eager to blow him at the party.

He doesn't dislike Chiara. As far as women go, and Moth has had a number of good female friends in the past, Chiara seems genuinely nice. It's not that he came over here with the intention of causing her harm.

However, burned into his memory are Arturo's jagged little words. How his rejection had slashed a vicious hole in Moth's heart, how the slurs were arsenic-coated spikes in his already wounded pride. He could vividly recall the shape of Arturo's lips as he called Moth a *fucking faggot.* Revenge tastes like candy. He is a monster.

Moth doesn't think. He puts his free hand on top of Chiara's.

The effect is immediate. Her pupils dilate, her breathing quickens, and her mouth goes slack. Her eyes become hazy with pleasure. Moth recalls how it felt when the Stranger touched him, that unrelenting and unquenchable sexual desire flooding all his senses. All of that he sees reflected in Chiara's face. She is a slave to it, under his control.

He sets the coffee cup down on the counter. He places his other fingers in her mouth, against her tongue. Her whole body shudders in a powerful orgasm that offers no release.

In Moth, the need has become painful. He's somewhat turned off by the idea of having sex with a woman, but he's done it before. He tells himself that he has to do this, that despite everything, he must survive.

And he knows that it doesn't have to be pretty or sweet or kind—out of necessity it can be quick and hard.

The dark thing inside him squirms, triumphant.

He dances his victim easily, gracefully into the bedroom.

~

Late evening.

Arturo locks up the law office after everyone else has gone home. In the parking lot, he leans against his car and calls Stefano. After some obligatory chitchat, Arturo casually asks if he'd like to grab a pizza. Stefano asks about Chiara. Arturo lies.

The truth is that Arturo is afraid of what will happen when he goes home. He'd ignorantly believed he could control it and was unprepared for the depth of his need, the one which threatened to engulf and consume him, nearly obliterating all restraint just from being next to her. He is a danger to her.

Stefano agrees to meet him in about an hour at the pizzeria near the park. Arturo snaps his phone shut then climbs into his car and drives toward the wall. He scores a spot in the nearby parking lot. Since he has time to kill, he heads down the hill towards the square. In the square he sees a cluster of junkies hanging out in front of the pharmacy. He notes that Moth is not among them, nor is the guy Arturo had met in the alley behind the gay club that night when he went looking for Moth.

One of the bars has tables and chairs set outside in the square. Since it's a beautiful night, Arturo opts to sit outside while he kills time with an *aperitivo*, watching the crowd,. By the time he finishes his drink, it's time to head back up the hill to meet Stefano.

They've only just ordered when Arturo regrets having invited Stefano to dinner. First of all, Arturo is finding it difficult to pretend that everything is all right. More importantly, the way Stefano is acting around him – like an awkward sixteen-year-old girl with a crush – is making him uncomfortable. It hadn't occurred to him that he would have this effect on other men, including his friends.

Arturo is tossed between a sea of anger and an ocean of despair. No girlfriend. No friends. He stands alone on a precipice watching as his whole world – his carefully constructed life – skews and skitters beyond his grasp.

Meanwhile, Stefano toys with his water glass, adjusts the silverware, trying not to brazenly stare at his friend who seems different to him somehow, brighter, more masculine, and just more put together than usual — and trying to hold up his end of the conversation.

It's too much for Arturo to bear. He leaves the table with the excuse that he has to call Chiara, and he does make a phone call in the restaurant's foyer, but to his parents, telling them to expect him tonight. He then returns to the table, apologetically explaining that he has to go, that Chiara needs him.

"No problem," Stefano says, with obvious relief. "Do what you have to do, man."

Arturo tosses down money, then beats a hasty retreat.

He knows that nothing will ever be the same. In the car, Arturo pounds the steering wheel with both fists, filled with a vague hatred aimed at the *fucking faggot* who turned his entire world upside down. He mourns the loss of his life; at the same time, he rebels against the idea that it's over. There has to be a solution. He will find it. He just needs time.

He drives home with the intention of picking up some things before spending the night at his parents' house, the only place he will be safe. As he climbs the stairs, he debates on what he will say to Chiara. He stops before the door, jangling his keys, still uncertain. Anxiety squeezes the heart in his chest and constricts his ribs, making it hard to breathe. Finally he manages to draw a deep, calming breath, and opens the door.

The lights are off. He switches on the nearest lamp. On the counter he spies Chiara's purse and jacket where she had left them earlier. An untouched espresso cup on a saucer. On the other side of the room, the bedroom door is open, spilling darkness.

He calls her name as he moves toward the bedroom. "Chiara…?

There's no answer.

Puzzled, Arturo stops in the threshold, peering inside, but unable to distinguish anything more than the indeterminate form of a body, motionless on the bed.

He reaches out a hand and flips the switch, flooding the nightmare with light.

~

Our protagonist steps out of the *tabacchi* into the night.

Standing at the edge of the street, he opens the pack of Marlboros he's just purchased with the cash pilfered from Chiara's purse. As he lights up, a group of teenagers push past, parting to flow around him like water. From the group, a burst of laughter snaps like a pop gun and then one of the boys tosses a glance over his shoulder back at Moth.

Moth takes a long drag off his cigarette. He doesn't care if they're laughing at him. He feels like he's on top of the world. Like he's grown wings and could fly like his namesake Michael, the archangel, all the way to the moon.

Smoking, he gazes up at the sky. Ambient city light masks the stars but from where he stands, he can see the moon waxing full. It soon occurs to him that he's standing in the street, not reciting poetry to himself as he often does, but staring at the moon like a true lunatic. Time to move on.

He starts walking. Walking feels good. How his limbs move, the slap of his boot heels on the stone, the gentle night air filtering over his face, the familiar burn of the nicotine-laced smoke in his lungs: all are marvelous sensations. Inside his velvet skin, his soul is light. His blood sings. He is grateful to be alive, grateful for all the beauty in the world — so alive, he feels no remorse for what he's done, and it is all clear to him now. He is, quite simply, a predator, and all of humanity his prey. It is survival of the fittest. The strong feed off the weak, the weak struggle against the strong, and everywhere there is conflict and strife. There is no good and evil; there is merely nature.

He walks to The Dive. Outside the door he lingers. The wind picks up, accosting him, prickling his skin, as the techno music from inside tickles his ears. Moth doesn't know exactly why he hesitates, as he has already decided that he will join Cristiano after all, at least for a while, and the best place to find him is still The Dive, assuming that Cristiano hasn't changed his mind about waiting for Moth's answer and already left town.

Perhaps Moth hesitates because there's always a good possibility that Orazio is inside, and Moth doesn't want to see him again. However, as he enters the club, he discovers that this fear is unfounded. No Orazio. It's still early, so there are only a few people scattered about the tables, no one on the dance floor, and no one he knows, including his Stranger. From habit, he checks his wrist, even though his internal clock tells him that it's just after eleven. His Movado reveals that it's precisely quarter past.

Moth finds a place at the bar and orders a drink. When the drink comes, he pays for it with a smile. Tracing the face of the watch, he thinks about his ex. He thinks about how, if they were to see each other now, Quentin would be unable to resist him. It's almost enough to make him want to return to Boston, this desire to use his power to have, once again, the man he still loves. It doesn't even matter to him that seducing Quentin would be tantamount to annihilating him, in one way or another, for a small and selfish part of Moth had always longed to destroy Quentin rather than see him happy with someone else.

Moth is so lost in this fantasy that the attack catches him off guard as a body suddenly slams into his, hands shoving, forcing him off the bar stool and up against the bar. A frenzy of punches, muted by the leather of his jacket, lands against his back and ribs before he can even think to turn around. Wedged between the bar and the stool, it takes him a moment to stumble free and face his attacker.

Arturo's face is contorted with rage. "You fuck!" he spits out, then renews his attack, managing a lucky punch to Moth's face.

This hurts. For the briefest of moments as he teeters back, Moth believes that his entire jaw has come unhinged from the force of the blow.

All around them, chairs go skittering back as the club's patrons close in, forming a circle around them. Moth pays them scant attention, instead focused on defending himself. He's never been much of a fighter, but when Arturo swings a fist at him again, Moth manages to block.

He seizes Arturo by the arm, lets him go again, and simultaneously shoves. Arturo stumbles back into the crowd. Some of the onlookers protest at being jostled, while others shout blood-thirsty words of encouragement. As they push him forward, back towards Moth, someone presses something into his hand.

A knife.

Arturo lunges forward, arm arching, knife rising. It happens so fast that Moth doesn't see the switchblade. He reaches out to tackle Arturo with the intention of wrestling him down to the floor, but Arturo twists his arm under Moth's own and thrusts forward with his fist.

There is little resistance as the blade sinks into Moth's abdomen, just below his ribs. Moth feels an odd twinge of pressure there but doesn't realize that he's been stabbed until Arturo jerks the knife back out. Flashing lights pulse over the blade.

Moth sees his own blood on it, and then the pain erupts, sizzling and sharp like a firecracker. He lifts a hand to his shirt, which is already sticky with blood.

Arturo, in a rage-fueled frenzy, arm upraised, lunges forward to strike again.

Moth attempts to dodge, but he isn't quick enough. The knife misses its target of Moth's chest but ends up implanted in Moth's thigh.

Moth thinks he screams but isn't sure if he actually makes a sound.

Arturo wrenches the knife loose and, in doing so, inadvertently slices Moth's femoral artery.

Many things happen at once. Blood jets out of Moth's thigh with the rapid rhythm of his heartbeat, at the rate of one-half liter per minute. Shock sends Moth sliding to the floor.

Arturo staggers back. On his face, an expression of disbelief. The knife slips from his hand and clatters across the floor. Arturo sinks down, utterly despondent, to his knees.

The bartender shouts, "I'm calling the cops!" and the crowd naturally disperses, everyone scrambling to grab their jackets and escape before the police arrive.

Only one man moves against the crowd. He steps over to Moth, kneeling down to press both his hands over the wound in Moth's thigh in an attempt to stop the bleeding. Blood oozes out from between the man's tan fingers and the reflection of the strobe lights flashing in his dark eyes. "It's going to be okay," Juan says over the music, pressing down harder.

Blood pools on the floor below Moth. Three minutes pass like three hours.

The police arrive first. Arturo does not resist arrest.

One cuffs him and hauls him up the stairs and out of The Dive into the waiting police car. Moth hopes that they lock him in a cell, all alone, for the next three or four days.

The other officer crouches down beside Moth. "Hang in there," he says. "An ambulance is on the way."

Two minutes pass like hours as Juan valiantly continues his attempt to staunch the flow of blood from Moth's thigh. Finally, the paramedics arrive. Juan's hands withdraw, new hands are applied, and Moth is rushed out of the club into the waiting ambulance. The sirens swirl, cutting through the night, as the vehicle bounces over the stones in Via Veneto towards the hospital, only minutes away.

One paramedic drives as the other tends to Moth in the back of the ambulance, trying to save his life. As the blood soaks through the wad of gauze, he adds another wad of gauze, then another and another. The paramedic turns his head, shouting over his shoulder to the driver. "Damn it, he's bleeding out!"

These are the last words that our protagonist ever hears. He finds them difficult to comprehend, and yet his final thought is that maybe he got what he deserved, what all monsters deserve in the end. The edges of reality flicker, then death folds him into her arms, carrying him down.

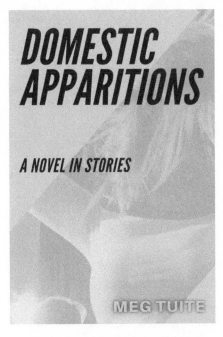

With a new epilogue for this second edition, Meg Tuite's Domestic Apparitions is a tour de force novel in stories about surviving Catholic girlhood and growing up in a neighborhood that both forces coming of age and probes the intricacies of codependent family tragedies. Exploring a childhood set in the late 1970's, this book takes our narrator on a journey of maturing into adulthood that changes her view on the past she barely escaped and catapults her into a future with new challenges to overcome. Tuite's incisive and searing writing makes this journey memorable and one a reader will not soon forget.

DISCARD

9 781734 305272